She stood on th  *und hesitantly.*

Dressed in a fancy black dress with a full skirt and a black, wide-brimmed hat with feathers, the woman met his gaze, and Cal felt a sudden jolt. Nobody dressed like this had ever come to Pell's Valley.

He hurried over and held out his hand. "Ma'am? Can I help you?"

Her blue-eyed gaze met his, and Cal swallowed hard. "Name's Cal Rutledge."

"And I'm Jessida Wilcox, but people call me Jess." She held out a gloved hand.

Jess? Had he heard correctly? Could this be the Jess he had written to? The sister of the woman he'd buried? The aunt of Charlie? But she couldn't have received his letter already. Why had she come?

"Why do you look so surprised?" she asked.

"Are you from Kansas?" Cal asked.

Her eyebrows rose. "Yes, I am, but how did you know?"

Cal shrugged. "I wrote to you on Monday."

BIRDIE L. ETCHISON hails from the southwest corner of Washington State, just two blocks from the ocean. She writes for pleasure and thanks God every day for her driving compulsion to put words on paper. It's a blessing to hear that a reader has enjoyed a book, and it is the impetus that keeps her writing. She enjoys writing a column for her church newsletter and loves to travel, which brings more fodder for stories. Baking is also a hobby. "On days when the muse doesn't come, I bake," she says. That's why recipes usually appear in her books!

Books by Birdie L. Etchison

HEARTSONG PRESENTS

Don't miss out on any of our super romances. Write to us at the following address for information on our newest releases and club information.

Heartsong Presents Readers' Service
PO Box 721
Uhrichsville, OH 44683

Or visit www.heartsongpresents.com

Sagebrush Christmas

Birdie L. Etchison

Heartsong Presents

In remembrance of Uncle Grant,
who loved the wide-open spaces in Eastern Oregon,
and to Gail Denham, who helped with research

A note from the Author:
*I love to hear from my readers! You may correspond with
me by writing:*

Birdie L. Etchison
Author Relations
PO Box 719
Uhrichsville, OH 44683

ISBN 1-59310-634-3

SAGEBRUSH CHRISTMAS

All scripture quotations are taken from the King James Version of the
Bible.

All of the characters and events in this book are fictitious. Any resem-
blance to actual persons, living or dead, or to actual events is purely
coincidental.

*Our mission is to publish and distribute inspirational products offering
exceptional value and biblical encouragement to the masses.*

PRINTED IN THE U.S.A.

prologue

Slipping out the door into the still, cold night, Abigail shivered as she headed for the barn. It was December, and a midday snowstorm had dumped several inches of snow. It lay in drifts where the wind sent it scattering.

She found a heavy coat in the barn and slipped it on. It barely covered her middle, large with child. Eight months, the way she figured it. She hadn't seen a doctor but knew the baby was healthy because it kicked constantly, keeping her awake at night.

Abby also found a muffler and wrapped it around her neck. Work gloves hung from another hook, and an old hat with earflaps covered her head.

She would saddle Mr. Stubblefield's oldest horse, stand on a box, and hope she could climb onto the horse's back. A little help would be nice; but she was running away, and nobody must know.

Abby slept a few hours in the barn and set out as the sun came over the eastern hills. She had no idea where she was going or what would happen when she arrived, but circumstances made her flee. To stay would be disastrous. She clutched a satchel in front of her and held it tightly. Her possessions. The only other thing that mattered was the small gold cross she wore around her neck. A gift from Papa long ago.

"Jess," she said aloud to the wind as the horse plodded south. "If only I'd listened to you. If only I was back home in Kansas. If only—." Tears stung her cheeks as she looked above. "O Lord, whatever happens, please protect my baby."

Abby had married Lenny Thorne in haste, and he'd brought her west. Last night she'd overheard him talking to the ranch hands.

"Look—I know I owe you money, so just take my wife in trade."

Her heart sank as she realized she was being sold to pay his gambling debt. He was a scoundrel and didn't love her, nor did he care about their baby.

Abby gripped the reins, barely able to see ahead of her with the snow swirling about in the high desert winds. She had been so happy when she knew she was going to have a baby, someone to love and to love her back. She kept a roof over her head by cooking and cleaning house for Mr. Stubblefield. He'd been kind, treating her as a father might. If only her husband had been as kind. Abby pushed the thought out of her mind. She couldn't bear to think of that now. She'd had enough pain in the year since coming to Oregon.

Abby rode until the sun rose high in the sky, finally leaving the Stubblefield ranch and crossing onto someone else's land. She had to go out of the way to find a spot where the fence was down. Weary from the ride, she saw a small shack ahead. She urged the horse on as she felt a sudden jab, and then wet warmth ran down her legs and into her boots. Another cramp hit, and Abby slid off the horse. Gasping for breath, she grabbed the small satchel with her belongings—though nothing was important except the letters—all that was left of her other world. Jess. Dear, sweet Jess who had loved her and warned her about Lenny. *"Don't go now, Abby. Let Lenny go first, then set up a house and send for you. Doesn't that make more sense?"*

Since when had Abby chosen the sensible route?

Another pain, worse than the two before, tore through her middle. She stumbled to the lean-to just as the horse turned and galloped off in the direction from which they'd come.

Abby was alone out here in nowhere land, and she realized now she was about to have her baby. Was it coming early, or had she miscalculated? She fell to her knees on the cold dirt floor and moaned. When another contraction hit, she gripped the cross around her neck, and the chain broke.

What would happen now? Would someone find them? She clenched her teeth as she removed a small, worn blanket from the satchel. She cried out with no relief from the pain. *O Lord, I know You're with me. Please forgive my sins. Please let my baby live. Please bring someone here.*

one

Patches of snow covered the ground, but the sky was a clear blue, the air crisp and smelling of sagebrush. The wind had died down to an occasional howl as it rounded a bend between two hills.

Cal Rutledge prodded Dover along. The trail was rocky in spots, but his five-year-old buckskin was sure-footed. He'd had Dover since before he married Millie. The memory of her brought a rush of feeling to the surface. He swallowed hard and let up on the reins.

"Well, boy, we've been through a few things together. Now we're starting a new adventure—ranching in Oregon. Do ya think we're up to it?"

Dover tossed his head as if he understood.

"Yep. That's the way I feel, too."

Cal looked out over his newly acquired ranch. He was five hundred miles from Montana, which had always been home. This Oregon land was his, but it would take a long time to forget the endless blue Montana sky and spring-green meadows where daisies grew in wild abandonment.

He pushed on, but he was in no hurry. He had nothing to go back to in town. Unless he counted a room over the noisy saloon—noisy on Saturday nights, that is. While cowboys drank and played poker and girls danced, Cal tried to sleep, tried to forget the memories. Once in a while he'd dig out Millie's worn Bible, the one treasure that had belonged to his wife. Millie had underlined several favorite passages. "It's not good to mark one's book," she'd said, her dark eyes snapping, "but I want to find a verse quickly when I need it."

Cal had memorized one of her favorites: "Rest in the Lord,

and wait patiently for him." Yet he found it difficult to be patient. Or to pray. When Millie lay dying and the doctor said there was no hope, he'd cried out that there had to be hope. There was *always* hope. But his prayers had gone unanswered. A year ago he'd buried her in the family plot in Montana, but he'd had no daisies to adorn her grave.

Cal shaded his eyes, looking as far as he could. He was in a canyon as hills rose to the east and south sides of his ranch. He thought now of the land he'd roamed as a lad, the time he'd chased the wild horses, learned how to rope a cow, brand a calf—all memories of life on his father's ranch. Now that belonged to his brother, and these thousand acres were his. He would call it Poplar Place because of the two stands of the stately tree. One was close to the remains of a chimney where a house had burned, and the other was several yards away. One day he'd build another house in that spot. Maybe, if his heart ever healed, he'd find a woman to share it with sometime.

A pond nearby would be a good watering hole for the cattle he'd soon have grazing on the range. Come spring he'd buy a few hundred head. Good thing he hadn't planned to farm, because he doubted wheat or corn could grow in this sagebrush-filled land, but *something* might grow here. He'd have to find out.

He stopped, noticing a shift in the wind. Nightfall happened earlier here, it seemed. If he plodded along much longer, he might not make it to town by dusk.

"Dover, I daresay a storm is brewing. Time to head back."

He rode on to the lean-to, something he'd noticed the first time out. Abandoned by an early settler, it offered a welcome change to the scenery.

A sudden yowl filled the still air. Cal drew in the reins. It sounded like an injured animal. Could there be an old trap inside the cabin that a coyote or wolf had tripped across? He remembered finding a trapped wolf one winter. His father told him to shoot it. "A wolf with a mangled foot would be no good in the wilds of a wintry Montana, Son."

The sound came again, louder, more persistent, and his heart lurched. This time it reminded him of his sister Loretta's boy, the night little Jacob came into the world. Cal had looked forward to hearing that same sound when his own child was born, but it wasn't meant to be. His son was stillborn after a long, difficult labor, and minutes later Millie had breathed her last. He remembered reaching over and closing her brown eyes, once filled with love for him. They would never look at him again. He swallowed hard, not letting the emotion take over.

Cal pointed Dover in the direction of the lean-to and dismounted. He felt for his gun in the holster. One never knew when a bobcat or mountain lion might attack in this desolate land.

He moved slowly through the doorway. It was dank and icy cold inside, with only a bit of daylight coming from one dirt-encrusted window. The frantic cry came again. Finally Cal's eyes adjusted to the dark, and he saw movement.

"Hello?" Cal ventured, coming closer.

A moan joined the cry. Cal bent down as a woman's hand flailed from a scrap of blanket.

"Oh, my, what have we here?" A baby had just been birthed. Cal would never forget the sight and smell of blood.

"Miz?" He reached for her wrist in hopes of finding a pulse. "I'm here to help. What's your name?"

Her fingers clutched his coat, and he leaned closer. Another lusty yell sounded. Tiny fists rose, as if in anger, seemingly gathering strength from somewhere. The young woman turned and stared out of vacant eyes. Her face was covered with dark, matted hair. She reached toward the baby. "Please," she whimpered, "please take care of my baby."

Cal took her hand and held it tight. "I'll help. Take deep breaths."

"Too—late." She sighed. "Find—Jess." Her hand slipped away

and lay limp as the wind howled around the shack, matching the baby's hungry cry.

O Lord, what am I to do? Jess? Who is Jess? And what about this little one?

Cal covered her face. Her suffering was over, but unlike the child of his Millie, this woman's child lived and would continue to do so if he could get back to town and find someone to wet-nurse it. He hadn't been in Pell's Valley long, but he'd heard Sarah Downing had a baby. Would she consider sustaining the life of this newborn?

Looking at the baby's smudged face, Cal pulled back the cover and saw it was a boy. His heart lurched again when he noticed the child was still attached to the afterbirth. He took out his pocketknife and rubbed it back and forth on his pants, then tied the cord and cut it, all the while thinking, *What am I to do with a child and a dead woman?*

The body had to be buried. If he didn't bury her, wolves would find her corpse—and he couldn't let that happen. Everyone needed a decent burial.

When Cal lifted her body from the blanket, a small packet tied with a ribbon fell to the ground. It looked like letters, and he saw the name "Jess" scrawled across the top envelope. He would take the letters, hoping to discover some clues. He had to find someone who wanted the child. *O Lord, let it be so.*

He then noticed a small gold cross on the woman's bosom, a broken chain clutched in her hand.

Minutes later, with the baby yowling in the background, Cal dug a small grave and tenderly placed the body in it. He considered putting in the cross but changed his mind. He'd add it to the letters for someone to claim. Cal covered the grave. He made a rectangle of stones and piled a snow-covered juniper branch on top. He took off his hat and laid it over his heart for a moment, then pulled out his Jew's harp and played "Jesus Loves Me." He hesitated a long moment before words came.

"Lord, I don't know this woman, but You do. In Your infinite grace You have taken her to be with You. May her soul rest in peace, and help this wee one live. In Your name. Amen."

Cal built a fire and removed the flannel shirt under his coat. The child was wet; he needed protection, and this would have to do for now. Wrapping the baby in his plaid shirt, he tried to get water inside his tiny mouth. He couldn't take much, but even a little bit might help.

After warming his hands, he placed the infant close to his chest and buttoned up his overcoat. The coat was too large because he hadn't eaten right since Millie's death. He climbed onto Dover, gave a last look toward the makeshift grave, and headed back to town. He hoped he would make it by dark and before snow began falling.

❧

Cal thought again of Millie as Dover trotted north toward town. He'd blocked some of the memory out, the mornings of turning to her side of the bed only to find a cold, empty space. He remembered getting up and making coffee, putting out two cups, two plates, and two sets of silverware.

"Lord, have You forsaken me?" he'd cried out more than once. "I can't go on like this. I hear her calling me; I feel her touch and see her braiding her hair."

He remembered the day his brother, Tom, came by, carrying a dead calf. "It was out there, waiting for you to come," Tom reproved, shaking his head. "I wonder how many more I might find."

"Then why don't you go back and look?" Cal yelled.

Tom turned and set the calf down. "I don't like saying this, Cal, but you gotta snap out of it. Millie's not coming back, and you know that. But life goes on, and you need to do something besides feeling sorry for yourself—"

Cal flung out his arm, knocking his brother off the step into a snowbank. He stood there and stared at him. Never had Cal struck out like this, and he felt instant remorse. "I—I—" But

Tom scrambled to his feet and took his horse at a run.

"Tom!" Cal called out, but his brother was gone, leaving the calf behind. He bent down, looking at the stiff calf, one that was not strong enough to make it in a Montana winter.

That day Cal knew it was time to move on. He talked it over with his brother, who bought him out, house, land, cattle, and all. Cal apologized for the fight, holding out his hand, but Tom didn't acknowledge his apology and turned away.

Most of that next year was spent wandering from town to town, not wanting to settle down, helping at a ranch here and there and then moving on. He arrived in Pell's Valley the second day of December 1899, with one horse, a bedroll, a change of clothes, and the saddlebag with provisions. Winter had hit this part of eastern Oregon with a vengeance. He wouldn't find much work, but surely someone would have a fence to mend, a building to erect. He stayed in this valley town, miles from the nearest town of any size, one of the last stops for the Union Pacific train. And then he'd found the land for sale and knew he would settle here. Maybe now he could put Montana and Millie behind him, though it seemed unlikely he'd ever stop loving her.

❧

The baby cried, bringing Cal back to the present. His whimper seemed to say, "I am hungry. Don't let me die."

A boy. Just like the one he'd lost. Cal hadn't pined for his baby as much as for his wife. After burying the two in the same grave on the north side of the property, he'd put a fence around the grave and carved her name on a stone. And then he'd wept as he never had before. The vivid memory haunted him every night. Now the dark-haired woman he'd buried only an hour ago crossed his mind. So young, like Millie. But she'd seen her baby alive, heard him cry, reached out and took his tiny hand.

Cal urged Dover on. They both must get back to safety before another snowstorm hit. There'd been one last night, and

Cal wondered how the young woman had found her way to the deserted shack. Someone had to have dropped her off, but who would leave a woman alone in the middle of nowhere? Had they known birth was imminent? He'd never find the answers unless they were revealed in the bundle of letters addressed to Jess. Was Jess the father of the child? A brother? A sister? He'd look for someone who knew the dead woman. And as the baby cried again, this time more of a whimper, Cal hit the reins. Dover tossed his head as if he knew time was important.

Words from one of Cal's favorite songs welled up inside him, bursting forth and filling the empty land with song. It was mournful, and he'd sung it before under different circumstances.

> *Oh, bury me not on the lone prairie,*
> *Where the coyotes howl and the wind blows free,*
> *In a narrow grave just six by three.*
> *Oh, bury me not on the lone prairie.*

This wasn't the prairie; but it was surely lonesome, and the coyotes howled every night. The baby was quiet, and a chill ran through Cal. Could he be dead? He stuck his hand inside, felt the heartbeat, and breathed a prayer of thanks.

❧

Darkness fell, and the first snowflake hit Cal's cheek as he arrived in town. The baby had not cried since the song. Cal supposed the constant motion of riding, similar to a rocking chair, had lulled the boy to sleep. *Charlie.* He had no idea what the baby's name would have been, but he had to have one. Everyone had a name, even an old cur dog. He picked Charlie because it was a good name and reminded him of his best friend from school days.

A whimpering began as Dover slowed to a trot.

"I know, I know," Cal crooned. He pushed his worn hat

back and felt the snow fall with sudden fierceness. "Charlie, you gotta make it. I didn't bring you all the way back here to have you die on me. And we'll find this Jess person. Yes, we've gotta do that."

The Downing house was at the east end of Main Street. A small house, he wondered how they could fit so many young'uns in it, but fit they must. He knew little about the family since they kept to themselves. Mr. Downing worked on the Stubblefield ranch. He'd seen him only once. If Mrs. Downing had any heart, she couldn't let a newborn die. Cal prayed she would be willing to help, and he intended to pay for her help. It was only right he should.

Cal dismounted, tromped up the steps, and took a deep breath before knocking. He heard scurrying sounds inside, then nothing. The door opened after his second knock.

two

"Jess, don't go." Brady's eyes, dark pools of brown intensity, pleaded. "You've been getting Abby out of trouble all her life. Isn't it time she started being responsible for her mistakes?"

Jessida Wilcox looked at the man who had helped her through the death of her parents. She was thankful he had been there—harvesting the crops, making sure she got the best price. She knew Brady loved her. Though he'd never said it, he showed it in many ways. Right now his gaze was steady. Searching. His expression revealed pain, and her insides quivered with guilt. She thought of a conversation with her grandmother once. Grandmother Wilcox, wise and pointed in her observations, said, "Jessida, one does not have to love to marry. Love comes later." While voicing her opinion, her grandmother never looked up from her knitting.

I could never marry unless I loved someone, she'd wanted to say. But the words stayed tight inside her. One did not argue with Grandmother.

As Jess recalled the vivid memory, she knew Brady was right. It was time for Abby to grow up, to live the life she'd chosen without help from Jess. But she couldn't admit he was right and she was wrong. "Jess, there's a stubborn streak in you a mile wide," Pa always said. She knew it to be true, but she was determined to have her way and so far had never met anyone who challenged it. Abby had, of course, but no man.

Jess lifted her chin. "But I must go, Brady. If I don't and something happens to Abby, I'll regret it the rest of my life, especially after making Mother that promise."

"Then let me accompany you—"

"No. I must do this alone. Besides, you need to take care of things here."

It was December, and harvest was long past. The remaining cornstalks, what hadn't been fed to the cattle, stood like sentinels in the fields. Fences needed mending, though, and Brady was busy working on the joint fence that separated their property.

"I wonder what it would be like to have a ranch out west," Brady had remarked just last week. "Might be nice."

"Can't imagine leaving here," Jess had answered. Now it looked as if she was about to find out.

"I'll bring Abby back if I have to hog-tie her," she said, her thoughts returning to the present. "She has to admit she made a mistake."

"Is it safe to travel out there where Indians might attack?"

"I understand they used to have problems, but the Indians are on reservations now, so stop worrying. The train will be safe."

Jessida felt a twinge of eagerness and slight trepidation at the thought of riding the train, of seeing Oregon, a land she'd only read about in books. The days of the covered wagon were long past, but she had heard that parts of wagons were abandoned along the trail and graves were scattered across the land.

"See you in the morning, Jess." Brady strode across the room and opened the door. "I'll be here early to drive you to the station."

Jess watched Brady leave. She should have called after him, but she sat motionless.

December. Christmas. Her mind went to Christmases in the past. The old farmhouse decorated with bells, garlands, and candles; a tree in the corner by the large window with an angel on top. Always they'd had ginger cookies and sugar cutouts she and Abby had decorated ever since she could remember. And her mother's favorite—a date-oatmeal bar cookie, all chewy and yummy. The scent of cinnamon and nutmeg filled the house for a week before Christmas. On Christmas Eve her father's big hands held the family Bible as he read the story from Luke. Later they joined their voices for "Hark, the Herald Angels Sing!" while her mother played the piano, and she sang out the loudest of all.

Jess swallowed hard. She never decorated as her mother had, though Abby used to beg her to. They baked cookies, but this year she had done nothing to prepare for Christmas. Without family it seemed pointless. She looked back at the closed door and felt a dull pain seep into her being.

Jess started packing for the journey. All she had was a small trunk and a valise. She'd never gone anywhere before and wondered what to take. Her new calico and the blue chambray with white lace collar, plus one of her older muslins, should be enough. She'd wear her best black bombazine for the train ride. It was the same dress she'd worn at Mama and Papa's funeral three years ago. The black hat with gray feathers would make her presentable, she hoped.

❧

Brady came early since it was a twelve-mile wagon ride to the station.

"You look beautiful," he said, placing her trunk in the wagon. When he went to help her, Jess had already climbed up.

"Thank you for the compliment, Brady."

"I've brought a gift." He withdrew a small box out of his overcoat pocket, and Jess felt guilty. She should have bought him some little remembrance. How could it have slipped her mind?

"I have nothing for you, Brady, not even the ginger cookies you like—"

"It doesn't matter." His hand touched her shoulder, and she liked the comfort it gave her. He was a good man. A strong man. Yet she didn't feel for him what he obviously hoped she would.

"Open this on the train and think of me. And"—he cleared

his throat—"please wear it every day."

"I will," she said, as the conductor called, "All Abo-o-o-oard!" She started up the steps. "And I will pray for you," Jess added.

Brady nodded but said nothing to acknowledge her last words. He was not a believer—the one flaw, a major one, in his otherwise sterling character. *How could he not believe?* she'd asked herself more than once.

Jess felt a twinge of sadness as she watched Brady from the window. He waved good-bye, and she fluttered her best lace handkerchief as the train chugged out of the station.

≈

Cal stood in the doorway holding the small bundle as silence surrounded the cabin.

"Yes?" Sarah Downing opened the door a crack and peered out, her eyes wary.

"I'm Cal Rutledge—"

She nodded. "Yes, I've heard the name." The door opened farther.

"I found this newborn out on my land. The mother died after giving birth." He thrust the bundle toward her. "I was hoping you could nurse the child."

Her face softened as she reached for the infant, and Cal saw two faces peering around a curtain in a far corner.

"I have a young'un of my own, but—" She pulled the blanket back and looked. His eyes were wide, and then he opened his mouth in a loud squall. "I 'spect he's hungry all right."

Cal left, reassured that Charlie was going to be okay. He wouldn't starve, and Mrs. Downing would care for him.

That night, back in his room on the top floor of the saloon, he opened the satchel. He set the cross aside and held a gold button in his hand. It was probably from a man's military uniform, and he wondered what significance it had. Obviously it was something that had meant a great deal to the young girl. He picked up the packet of letters and slipped off the ribbon. He discovered her name was Abigail, but she was most often called Abby in the letters from Jess. Cal had to get in touch with this Jess Wilcox. The address was blurred, but he made out a postmark from Oberlin, Kansas. He'd write a letter tonight and hope the town was small enough for the postmaster to know where the Wilcox family lived.

❧

The journey would take three days and nights. Jess had brought her Bible, a small diary to write her thoughts in, and hard candy, a gift Brady said she needed for the trip. She also had the little package he'd just given her. Jess knew it wasn't a ring; the box wasn't the right size. It was probably a necklace or a bracelet. She didn't want to open it yet but would save it for later.

She remembered that Abby, in her youthful exuberance, begged each Christmas Eve to open just one gift early. And her mother always gave in. Jess, being older, waited until Christmas morning because that was the rule, and rules weren't to be taken lightly.

As the train passed flat open prairies and farmlands, mountain ranges covered with snow, then more farmlands, Jess wondered if there would be snow in eastern Oregon. She imagined so as Abby wrote that it was hillier than Kansas, with sagebrush and juniper everywhere you looked.

Jess withdrew Abby's last letter and read it twice.

Dear Jess,
  Things are not as I'd hoped. Lenny is gone most of the time. I don't think he loves me anymore, and I want to come home. Of course I need money—

There was more, but she couldn't read it again. Abby sounded desperate. Contrite. Soon Jess would be there to help straighten things out and bring her sister home. Abby had been a handful from the start. When their father was alive, he'd held the upper hand and Abby had behaved out of a sense of respect, but she did not show that same respect to Jess.

Jess recalled the tragedy—the wagon overturning, her parents dying. The brief service, which should have offered solace, had not.

"The Lord giveth, and the Lord taketh away," the preacher said. He'd said other things, but Jess's mind had wandered.

So much had happened with no time to prepare. Did anyone ever have a chance to prepare? At least her parents were in God's hands now, and with that thought Jess carried on, making the necessary decisions.

The farmland would be leased. Brady was only too happy to add to his acreage. Jess would receive profits from her share while he got a percentage. She knew Brady wanted the Wilcox land; he'd approached her father more than once, offering to buy. Her father had always said no, just as she later said no.

❧

Her thoughts turned to Abby again. At seventeen she ran off with a man she met in town. With dark hair and eyes that didn't meet your gaze, he wasn't the sort of person Jess would have chosen for Abby—not that her sister would listen to reason. All she talked about was going to Oregon. "Wide open spaces is what Lenny says. One can make lots of money there."

With a satchel, a carpetbag, and a sack containing lunch, Abby and Lenny had boarded the Union Pacific train heading west. Abby had run back down the steps, leaned over, and kissed Jess's cheek. "Now don't you worry none."

"You could at least get married first," Jess said, her chin jutting forward. If only she had Papa's clout and could talk her sister into thinking this over.

"We did yesterday."

"You *did*? But where, and why wasn't I invited to the ceremony?"

" 'Cuz you would have insisted on me marrying in a church,

and there wasn't time. The JP said the words over at the county courthouse."

Two months later Jess received the first letter. She was frantic by then and had leaned on Brady. He'd stop by often and come in for a cup of coffee and one of Jess's homemade cinnamon rolls.

That first letter was now on the bottom of the stack of letters. The young couple soon discovered that Hampton, Oregon, was not farmland after all. Nothing but sagebrush and more sagebrush. It was good for cattle, but that took money, and Lenny had none. But he "has ways of getting the necessary funds," Abby continued. "Don't you worry, Jess. I'll keep in touch.

"It was such a hot summer, just like in Kansas, but it seems I don't perspire as much. It's dry here. The townsfolk say it will snow all winter long."

They moved to a place called Pell's Valley, with Lenny promising they would return to Kansas as soon as he made enough for the train tickets. But he liked to gamble, and one night he lost their meager savings in a poker game.

"He left me, Jess, but I'm okay. I'm helping a rancher with the cooking because his wife died. I'm saving money to come home to Kansas."

Jess straightened her shoulders. Abby had written one last letter, saying she had a secret and could Jess send her the needed funds to make the trip home? But she'd not included the address, and Jess hadn't sent money. It was as if God told her she must go to Oregon to see for herself what sort of trouble Abby was in. Together they could return to Kansas. She thought of Brady again and knew she should just sell him the farm and go on to teach school as she'd planned to do before her parents died. She didn't have the heart for farming.

Jess reached for her Bible and read Psalm 139. The next-to-last verse always gave peace to her troubled soul. "Search me, O God, and know my heart: try me, and know my thoughts."

She closed her eyes as the train sped over the miles, and soon darkness fell.

It was a fitful night. A child cried up the aisle a ways, but everyone else appeared to be sleeping. If only Jess could sleep. She thought of the last time she and Abby had attended the small church in town. Abby had protested about going as she protested about everything. Jess didn't understand her little sister. Why did she balk at the rules? Why had she turned from church and God's love? What could Jess have done differently? She trembled as a chill hit.

"Excuse me, miss, but would you like a blanket? I have two." The lady across the aisle smiled and offered a small patchwork quilt.

"Oh, I—oh, my, yes. But how did you know?"

"The Lord told me you were in need of one."

Jess smiled as she held the quilt close. "It's so kind of you."

She wanted to say more, but the lady had turned back, her head resting on the pillow. Jess did the same, the colorful covering warming her lap and legs. *God heard my plea, without my uttering a prayer.*

☙

It was morning, a bright, clear day, when the train whistle tooted one long blast as it pulled into the station. Jess bolted up, realizing she'd finally fallen to sleep. She patted her curls and straightened her hat. "Where are we?" she asked.

"This is Pell's Valley," the lady said, "and it's where I get off."

Jess handed the quilt back. "Me, too. And thanks so much for letting me use this."

"You're welcome, child. Now why are you here?"

"I've come to take my sister back to Kansas."

"Blessings on you, child."

Jess gathered her things and looked out the window. Was this the town? She saw a few buildings, but nothing as she expected. The whistle blew twice more and lurched, sending soot throughout the car. Jess gasped, covering her face too late.

She looked out again at the bare, flat land. No wonder Abby had been unhappy. As soon as she found her, they'd be on the next train heading out. They would make it back in time for Christmas. Wouldn't Brady be surprised?

The door opened, and Jess waited a moment. She was in no hurry, and yet she felt a sense of impending doom, a feeling she couldn't quite shake. Two men greeted the older lady, and Jess wished someone were there to meet her.

❧

Cal always met the train, especially if he had something coming in. He'd hitch the wagon to Dover and go the two blocks to the station. The train announced its arrival, and the townspeople came to greet others or to see what the train had brought. Supplies for the general store and the saloon always came in, and sometimes cattle and chickens, and last week there had been geese. Cal wondered about raising geese but didn't know enough about this area yet.

Cal didn't have much to keep busy with during winter. He'd hired out at a ranch west of town; but the fences were mended, and until the heifers gave birth, he wasn't needed. That left time to read, visit the baby, help the storekeeper on occasion, and meet the train. If the weather improved, he might start building on his property. He certainly needed a house. It didn't need to be a big house; a few rooms would do.

Some weeks nobody got off the train, but this Friday was an exception. Two young men met an older woman, and just as Cal was about to ask the conductor if his order was on the train, he saw her.

She stood on the top step and looked around hesitantly. Dressed in a fancy black dress with a full skirt and a black, wide-brimmed hat with feathers, the woman met his gaze, and Cal felt a sudden jolt. Nobody dressed like this had ever come to Pell's Valley.

He hurried over and held out his hand. "Ma'am? Can I help you?"

Her blue-eyed gaze met his, and Cal swallowed hard. "Name's Cal Rutledge."

"And I'm Jessida Wilcox, but people call me Jess." She held out a gloved hand.

Jess? Had he heard correctly? Could this be the Jess he had written to? The sister of the woman he'd buried? The aunt of Charlie? But she couldn't have received his letter already. Why had she come?

"Why do you look so surprised?" she asked.

"Are you from Kansas?" Cal asked.

Her eyebrows rose. "Yes, I am, but how did you know?"

Cal shrugged. "I wrote to you on Monday."

three

"You wrote me a letter?" Jess's eyes widened. "But you don't even know me, unless—" Her blue eyes widened. "It's about Abby, isn't it?"

The knot in his throat kept Cal from answering.

How can I tell this young woman her sister is dead?

He momentarily forgot he'd come to see if the train had brought his supplies. Forgot Dover waited with the wagon. Forgot he'd seen Charlie earlier that day, holding him close. All he could think about was this woman standing before him and knowing he'd be the one to give her the devastating news.

"So how do you know Abby? And where is she? Please take me to her."

"She's not exactly here," Cal finally said, "but she left something for you—"

"Left something for me? But she's not here?" Jess's eyes blazed with sudden anger. "You mean that scoundrel took her off someplace else?"

Cal looked at the soft golden hair that hung in ringlets, framing a round face. How different from the young woman dying in the shack. He thought about Charlie over at the Downings'. Within a short time he had grown to love the baby.

"No, he didn't take her anywhere."

"So where is she then?" Jess's voice rose with impatience. "I demand to know. You must take me to her."

She left you a special gift you'll like, Cal wanted to say.

"Can we go now? That is, if you don't mind."

"I have to unload supplies from the train," Cal said. "Please wait a minute while I pack them onto my wagon."

26

"And there's my trunk," Jess added. "Perhaps you would get that also."

"Yep," Cal said, noticing the trunk on the platform. "I'll get it."

"I've waited this long, so what's a few more minutes?" Jess said.

She looked at him with obvious puzzlement. He had to tell her. He had no choice. She would probably shed tears, and Cal had never managed tears well.

It took three trips to the wagon, and then he rejoined Jess, who was making a face.

"I can certainly see why Abby wanted to come home. Is there anything but sagebrush here? And where is the *real* town?"

"This *is* Pell's Valley," Cal said. "It's spread out a bit, but most of it's right here on this street."

"Oh, surely not." Jess shook her head. "I don't see anything but two gray buildings and the train station. Where is the church? The school?"

"Ma'am," Cal said, "we don't have a church, and no school either, though there's been talk of one."

"No church?"

"We'll get one someday."

"And the wind," Jess continued, holding on to her hat. "Does it always blow like this?"

Cal nodded. "Yep. And it snows a lot, too."

She adjusted her hat. "Yes, I can see that."

"You'll probably be heading back on the next train," Cal said. Clearly there was nothing to keep the woman here.

"Yes, after I see Abby."

"It'll be a week before the train comes again."

"So I'll need to stay somewhere, and where might that be?"

"There's a boardinghouse down the road apiece. I'm sure Emma can put you up. It won't be fancy though."

"Fancy isn't necessary, I assure you."

He nodded. "Guess anyone can manage for a short while." Cal stared at the woman who looked at him now with a bit of defiance. She tapped her foot. He laughed inwardly at the shoes, fancy with silver buckles and high heels, totally inappropriate for the wilds of eastern Oregon. How could he tell her he had buried Abby out in a stand of sagebrush with a sprinkling of rocks to let people know it was a grave?

"Let's go," Cal said. "It's just down the street—that last house."

"May I pay you for your trouble?"

Cal shook his head. He would never take money for helping another. His mother—God rest her soul—would have booted him good if he'd taken money for doing someone a favor. Favor? Burying a young woman was more than a favor, but when you had no choice, you did what you had to do.

"Come." Cal walked to the other side of his wagon, and Jess followed. She was taller by half a head. Cal was used to it, being short all his life. Livvy, who worked in the general store, was more his size, and she kind of liked him. But Cal was not looking for anyone. Not now. Not ever. Millie had been his life. He could never replace her or fill the hole in his heart.

Jess said nothing as Cal assisted her onto the wagon seat. He wished he'd brought a blanket, but this would have to do. He handed her the valise, and she thanked him.

Dover plodded down the dirt street, rutted from wagon wheels and buggies. "You'll like Emma over at the boardinghouse. She's a good cook."

He gave Jess a sideways glance, expecting her to talk, but she stared straight ahead, tight-lipped. Cal welcomed the silence, since so far all she'd done was complain.

When they reached the boardinghouse, the door opened before they stepped onto the porch.

"Well, Cal Rutledge," Emma said, her cheeks round and rosy. "You've brought someone from the train."

Cal removed his hat and let Jess go in first. "Yep. This lady has come to find her sister—" He shook his head at Emma, thankful Jess was looking around the room. He wanted her to know about Abby when the time was right, and that wasn't now.

"I see."

"As soon as I take her trunk to her room, we'll go to the Downing house."

Emma smiled. "Howard can take the trunk, Cal. That's his job."

"Perhaps you'd like to rest a bit," Cal began.

"It'd only take a minute to fix a cup of tea," Emma interrupted, "and I have freshly baked cookies—"

"I think not," Jess said. "I came to find my sister, and nothing else is important."

"Very well." Cal put his hat back on. "We'll be on our way then."

Emma handed Cal a blanket. "You must plan on staying for supper tonight."

❧

Ten minutes later Cal pulled up in front of the small Downing home. He'd gone as slow as he could, dreading what had to be. He paused. It looked barren, and he wondered what Jess was thinking. After knocking, he heard noises and knew the children were hiding. They were like wild animals, afraid to talk to anyone.

He called out, "It's Cal Rutledge, Miz Downing."

The front door opened, and Sarah nodded. "Come in."

"Brought someone to see Charlie."

A second later, the child, wrapped in the soft blue blanket Cal had bought, was in Sarah's arms. She held him out to Jess. "You must be the aunt then."

"Aunt? But I don't—" And then her mouth formed a small *o*.

"This is your nephew," Cal said.

Jess held the child with awkwardness, as if she had never held one so young. "Abby's baby?"

"Yep."

"You're sure?"

"Yep, sure am."

"But how, and where is. . ." Her voice trailed off, and Cal knew she'd figured it out. By Abby's absence Jess had to realize Abby was gone.

"Abby's dead, isn't she?" Jess's face showed no emotion, but Cal noticed her hand shaking.

"Yes, ma'am, that she is." He bent the brim of his hat and looked away.

"And nothing could be done for her?"

"She was almost dead when I found her. If it hadn't been for young Charlie yowling, I'd have ridden on by without knowing she was there."

The Downing children watched and listened from the other room of the small, crowded shack.

"How did she die?"

Cal stuck his hat on his head and removed it again. This was hard. He didn't want to talk about it here, not in front of the Downing children.

"I'll tell you when I take you back to the boardinghouse."

Jess opened her mouth to protest, then stopped.

Cal put his hat back on. "I'll be outside."

He opened the door and stepped out. He couldn't stay in there anymore. He would take Jess out to the grave, if the snow let up, so she could at least pay her respects. For now she had something of her sister to love, to cherish. They'd talk tonight about Abby, and in the morning he'd give her the satchel with the packet of letters and trinkets.

He walked around outside the cabin, his shoulders hunched over against the wind. Walking was a way to think and work things through. Looking at Jess Wilcox made him angry; yet he felt something he didn't want to feel, and it scared his inner being. *O Lord, You know my heart, my inside and out. I can't take another disappointment. Help!*

❧

Jess fought to hold back the tears as she held the tiny infant close. He had Abby's eyes, big and dark, filling a heart-shaped face. He was tiny and so precious. She had Cal to thank for her nephew's survival. Why had he walked out just now? She looked toward the door.

"Mr. Rutledge, he comes every day," Sarah Downing said. "I took to the little guy right off. He needed milk, and I didn't mind none. What's a body good for if he can't help someone out?"

"I can never repay you." Jess touched the other woman's arm.

"No need to think of that."

"I'll be taking Charlie back to Kansas with me—when the train comes in again."

"Figured you'd probably be a-doing that." Sarah shook her head, putting her arm around a child who looked to be two or three years old. "Mr. Rutledge sure will miss the young'un."

"And how old is the baby?"

Sarah thought for a moment. "I don't rightly recollect—"

"Almost two weeks," a voice said from behind the curtain.

Sarah smiled. "Ya. That's my oldest boy. He keeps track of such things."

Two weeks. Jess understood now how the cowboy had grown attached to the baby whose life he'd saved.

"I want to come every morning to see him," Jess said.

Sarah Downing nodded. "That's fine, miz. Very fine."

"I can't believe Abby is dead." Jess said, her eyes blurring. "I should have come sooner. If she'd had medical attention, she might be alive now."

Sarah leaned over and patted Jess's shoulder. "You have him now."

The woman's full-skirted muslin was faded and stretched at the seams, though Jess assumed the garment had once been bright blue and fitted. Jess took her hand and squeezed it.

"And I have you to thank, Mrs. Downing, for keeping this precious baby alive." She bit her lower lip to keep from crying. Pa had taught her not to let her emotions show in front of people. It was difficult at times, but she remained strong and determined and knew Pa would be happy she carried on the Wilcox name well.

One of the younger girls peered around her mother's skirt. Her wide eyes looked at Jess as if she couldn't believe anyone so elegant could be sitting in the only easy chair in her house.

"Mary, put a stick of wood in the stove and put the teakettle on. I believe we have some tea left."

"Yes, Ma."

More faces appeared, and Jess gasped out loud. "Oh, my, you have a large family, Mrs. Downing."

Sarah nodded. "Many mouths to feed."

Jess didn't have much, but there was the money from her parents' insurance. This woman had saved her nephew. He was all she had left of her family, and for that she could never repay the debt; but she could see that this family had food in the cupboards and possibly a new dress for Sarah.

"Where did Mr. Rutledge go?" Jess asked, realizing Cal hadn't come back in.

"He's jest outside," a young voice piped up. A small child with a smudged face peered around a curtain that portioned the house off into bedrooms. Jess wondered where they all slept. So far she had counted six children, not including the baby in another cradle.

"Perhaps you might ask him to come in?"

The child darted to the door, making sure he didn't get too close to Jess. A minute later Cal walked into the room, taking off his hat.

"You wanted me?"

Jess looked up, her heart suddenly doing strange things. How could that be? *I don't even know this man. He found me a place to stay and brought me here to Abby's baby. I'm just feeling gratitude, but he seems concerned. Kind. Yet he won't talk about things, and I need to know more about Abby's last moments on earth. What will he tell me, and when?*

"I didn't want you waiting around for me," Jess said. "I'm going to have some tea with Mrs. Downing and hold the baby a bit longer."

"Charlie," Cal interjected. "Every livin' thing needs a name."

"Charlie?" Jess's dark blue gaze met his and held it. "Oh, yes, you're right, of course. Charlie it is. For now."

"Yep."

Jess looked back into the tiny face. He yawned and opened his eyes then.

"He's hungry," Sarah said. "I feed him about this time. Mary can fix our tea."

"I'll wait," Cal said, a determined look on his broad face. "You have no way to get back to Emma's."

"Surely they have a wagon here."

Sarah shook her head. "Elias—my husband—has it. Don't know when he'll be back."

"Very well," Jess said. "Give me ten more minutes."

Jess handed the baby over, contemplating the name Charlie. Charles, of course. She didn't like nicknames. She always preferred Abigail to Abby, yet liked to be called Jess, not Jessida.

"And I will consider the name," she said, avoiding Cal's gaze as he stood at the door.

"Thank you."

❧

Cal walked out as a whoosh of wind came in behind him. The baby would always be Charlie to him, but of course he wouldn't be around long. Jess would take the boy back to Kansas. Nothing to keep her here. There she had family. Here life was rough. And she had already complained about the town's smallness, the fierce, cold air. No, he couldn't imagine her wanting to stay here in Pell's Valley.

It was cold, but Cal was used to cold. He dressed for it, something Jessida Wilcox needed to do. He doubted she had anything warm—considering that fancy black dress she was wearing.

The door finally opened, and Jess stepped out.

"I'm glad you waited."

"Couldn't do much else."

Cal helped her into the wagon for the third time that day.

"I'll be returning to Kansas with my sister's child on the next train."

"Yep. Figured as much." He picked up the reins and called, "Giddy up!" to the buckskin.

Jess's hand touched his shoulder. "Tell me now. I'm strong. How did she die?"

Cal stuck his hat on his head and removed it again. This was hard. He didn't want to talk about it or remember it, as it took him back to another time; but Jess needed an answer, and he was the only one to give it. And how could he still the pounding of his heart when she looked at him out of those blue eyes with the sun shining down on her golden curls?

"She didn't hurt anymore," he finally said.

"She talked to you?"

"Yep. Asked me to watch out for her baby. And"—he looked away, remembering the voice he could barely hear—"she said, 'Find Jess.'"

Jess's voice cracked. "Abby was all I had left in the world. I loved her so much, but we weren't on the best of terms when she left Kansas. If only I'd sent money when she first asked me—"

"Sometimes these things happen."

"It's a good thing our mother is gone. This knowledge would have killed her."

"I'm sorry," Cal said. He had the sudden urge to put his arm around the young woman but dismissed the idea as quickly as it had come. *How could I even think such a thing when I lost my*

Millie barely a year ago?

"I buried her," Cal said softly.

"You *buried* her?"

"Well, ma'am, one cannot leave a body in the desert. Not even in winter. Wolves come and take it—"

Jess held up her hand. "Let me think on that for a minute. Abby is buried somewhere in the desert?"

"I know where. It's on my land."

"Then you can take me there." Jess touched Cal's arm again. "Please don't think me ungrateful. I can never pay you for saving my nephew's life, and I do believe God sent you there that day."

Cal swallowed. "Yep, that's the way I see it."

"But I must go to her, pay my respects. Maybe we can take a preacher along to say a few words."

Cal wondered how—when the closest preacher was probably fifty miles away.

"I said a few words—uh, prayers, that is."

Jess shivered then, and Cal spoke without thinking first.

"Hope you brought something more serviceable to wear around here."

"What I wear is *none* of your business—" Jess stopped in midsentence. "Of course I didn't know the wind would be so bitterly cold."

"Bet Emma has a heavy coat that might fit."

Jess looked away, her chin trembling. "It's hard to imagine my sister being buried with nobody present and no service." She sighed. "But she's with our parents now, that is, if she came to the Lord before her untimely death."

"Couldn't say on that," Cal murmured.

"Abby was raised in church but went her own way the last few years."

Cal said nothing, and soon they were back at the boarding-house. Howard came around the side of the building and helped Jess down.

"You're staying for supper, Mr. Rutledge. Miz Emma asked me to remind you."

Cal wanted nothing more than to have some of Emma's wonderful cooking, but he couldn't bear to be around Miss Jessida Wilcox a moment longer.

"I'll come another time, Howard." He held out his hand to the young man. "Please thank Emma for me."

"Will do, sir."

Cal turned after bidding Jess a good evening. Even the noise of the saloon was better than her icy stares and the tears that brimmed in her deep blue eyes. He had to be alone to think.

four

Cal knew the ways of women. His mother had talked so sweetly to Pa, and Pa always seemed to do what she wanted. But Pa *wanted* to do it. And it had been the same with Millie. She'd look at Cal with those dark eyes and that fetching smile, knowing he'd bring her the stars if he could.

Jessida Wilcox smiled in the same way, but her manner was demanding. His mother used to wait a week for his father to see how it had to be. But Jess wanted things done *now*. He had a feeling it would be a long week.

❧

Jess went to her room to freshen up. Here in the solitude of her room she could cry. But the tears wouldn't come now. She removed the pins and placed her hat on a hook beside the oval mirror. Her hair, always curly, sprang free, and she ran her hand through it, reliving the awful thing that had happened to Abby. She couldn't erase it from her mind.

O Lord, she was alone. Out in that awful, barren spot—I don't know for sure that it's barren, but if it looks anything like this town, it is.

Jess thought of the beautiful cemetery back home, the surrounding cedar trees and wild flowers that bloomed each spring. It was a beautiful resting place. Here Abby was buried with no one present who knew or loved her. *How can I ever forgive myself?*

She lifted her chin and looked out the window. She knew some things would never be understood. God allowed things to happen, and Jess had a new life to live. She would be a mother to her nephew, the best one she could be. With Brady's help. . . Her heart tightened as Brady's face didn't come to mind; it was that cowboy who sprang to her thoughts. How could it be? She'd only met him, and he had a way of rankling her, of making her say things in a sharp way. And she didn't know why. That's what bothered her more than anything. *I don't know why.* She had dated a few men in her twenty-four years and knew Brady Hollingsworth loved her; but she had never, not even once, had this fluttery feeling she felt now.

She hung her chambray and a calico, then unfolded the faded brown muslin. It looked as if it belonged here. She was glad she'd packed it at the last minute.

Taking a deep breath, Jess stepped into the dress, pinned her hair back into place, and pinched her cheeks for color. Taking one last look at the gingham curtains and matching bedcover, she opened the door and walked down the steps. She'd get through this week somehow. And then she'd leave Pell's Valley behind and the grave of her little sister. It had to be that way. There was no other choice.

❧

The night was a restless one for Cal. The saloon noise and the loud voices in the hall didn't bother him, and that was unusual. He walked to the window and looked out, noticing the snow falling. It was December, after all. Of course they would have snow. He let the curtain fall back and walked to the bed, then back to the window.

Why can't I squelch my thoughts? Why do I keep thinking about Charlie and the way Jess looked holding him? Why did her blue eyes melt my soul?

He was thankful for his land, for the ranch he would have one day. Come spring he'd have cattle. He would have lots of work to keep him busy, to make him forget a baby boy and the woman who came and claimed him.

❧

A frantic knocking on his door awakened Cal. "What's going on?" he asked, opening his eyes.

"It's that lady a-asking for you," the voice said.

Howard. But what is he doing here? He opened the door and peered out.

Howard stared at Cal out of dark, bewildered eyes. "Miss Emma said I should come."

"Is it morning?"

"Yes, sir, but it's still dark out."

"Yep, so I see."

"And is it snowing?"

"Yes, it is."

"Then I'm going back to sleep."

"But Miz Wilcox—she's up and ready to go."

"Ready to go?" Cal's brain didn't work until he'd had some coffee.

"To the grave site."

Cal nodded and assured Howard he'd be along shortly.

"One more thing," Howard added. "She wants that satchel with the letters."

"Yep. Forgot about that. I'll bring it."

There she is, demanding again. Doesn't wait to see what I might do. No, it's gotta be the way she wants it.

Cal grabbed the satchel and minutes later saddled Dover and headed to the boardinghouse. He may as well have it out here and now. Snow covered the road, clung to the side in drifts, and the white stuff kept coming down, blowing right in his face. They'd make no ride to the grave site this day.

Jess was at the table when Cal entered. He smelled coffee and was thankful.

"Oh, there you are, Cal." Emma poured a cup automatically.

Jess rose out of her chair and stood in front of him.

"Here are the letters and trinkets, Miz Wilcox."

She took the satchel, her lip trembling. "Mr. Rutledge. Thank you for remembering. Now, about visiting Abby's grave—I won't rest a second until I've done that."

Her voice could have a gentler tone, Cal thought. He pulled out a chair. "Can't."

"Can't or *won't?*"

There it was again, that snappy way of talking. He felt as if he was one of her servants, and he didn't like it. She was spoiled, used to getting her way for sure, not sweet and loving like his Millie.

Cal narrowed his eyes and stared back. "Both."

"Both?" Her voice raised an octave.

"I won't because I can't."

Jess put her hands on her hips, and he couldn't help noticing how small her waist was. "Would you please not speak in riddles?"

Cal started to smile, a teasing kind of smile. No use in making her mad. She'd gone through a lot, after all.

"I can't today because a snowstorm is blowing out there, in case you hadn't noticed. And I won't until the weather permits."

"But it will be nice once the sun is up." Jess shot him a pleading look.

"Yep, but it's going to snow all day. I can tell."

"When then? Perhaps tomorrow?"

"We'll have to wait and see."

"And what about the baby's father?"

"Last I heard, Lenny Thorne was working at Stubblefield's— he owns the ranch next to mine."

"I must find him—we need to talk before I head back to Kansas with the baby—Charlie, that is." Jess stood, picking up her plate. "I'm willing to pay you for your time."

Cal turned away, not answering. There was that money issue again. Was that the way they handled things in Kansas? Friends didn't help friends? What sort of man would take money from a grieving woman? Not him, that was for sure. The only pay Cal wanted was for Charlie to stay in Pell's Valley. And if Jess stayed, he guessed that would be okay. Their paths wouldn't have to cross that much. He could stay out of her way. But a helpless feeling came over him, and he wasn't sure he wanted to do that. She had a determined manner. Sometimes that was good. Sometimes it was very good.

"I'll see what I can find out about Lenny Thorne." Cal pushed back his chair. "Thanks for the coffee and grub, Emma." He nodded at Jess. "I'll get back to you when I find out something."

"I guess that will have to do," she said.

🙟

Cal didn't want to drive all the way out to Stubblefield's, not with the weather as it was, so he decided to ask at the saloon about Lenny. He didn't like the saloon, but it was the only available room in Pell's Valley when he'd arrived. Emma kept her rooms at the boardinghouse for people staying a short spell. Cal didn't like the loud music and dancing. He couldn't look at another woman in that way. And he never had been one to gamble. His mother would turn over in her grave if she saw him gambling. It just wasn't done in the Rutledge family. They were God-fearing people, and Cal knew he would be God-fearing till the day he died. He might not pray as much as he should, and of course since Pell's Valley didn't have a church, he hadn't been to a service in several months. But he had Millie's Bible, and he often read a passage when he was out on his land alone. Communing with nature seemed to be the only way he could find God right now.

Nobody knew Lenny's whereabouts, except Florence, the girl running the operation. "Heard he went down to Calyfornia in search of gold."

Cal shook his head. "Thought they got all that gold by now—"

Florence smiled as she polished the bar. "Probably have, cowboy, but some men are fools, you know?"

Yeah, Cal knew all right. Maybe it was better Lenny Thorne was gone. That meant nothing was keeping Jess Wilcox here and she would take Charlie back to Kansas soon. The very thought almost tore his heart out. If only he could think of a way to keep Jess here—but he didn't know what it would be. He knew of no reason for her to want to stay. No, he'd be saying good-bye to the beautiful young woman and her nephew by the time the train came in next Friday.

Shoving his hat back on, Cal stalked out of the saloon, ignoring Florence's question about coming in later to see the show.

Cal felt sudden loss as he sauntered to the general store. He needed to buy a few supplies to take the next time he went out to his ranch.

five

It snowed Sunday, Monday, and Tuesday with a howling, bitter wind that pierced right through the bones. The snow blew into piles against fences, clung to rooftops, and heaped up in front of the Downings' home. As much as Jess didn't want to admit it, she could see what Cal meant. One could get lost in such a blizzard. She had stayed in the boardinghouse each day, only venturing out by midafternoon. She had to get over to see Charlie. *Charlie.* She wasn't sure the name fit him, but Cal had already named him, so how could she call him something else? She would once she returned to Kansas, but for here he would be simply Charlie.

"You aren't going out, are you, Miss Wilcox?" Emma cleared the lunch dishes off the huge round oak table in the dining hall. "It's too dangerous to be out and about. I don't know about Kansas, but here people get lost and are found a week later frozen solid."

Jess nodded. "Yes, I know, but I want to see my nephew."

"Perhaps it will be better tomorrow."

"You prefer I not take the wagon then?"

"Aye. You could, or I could have Howard take you, but it'd be better to stay here by the warm fire." Emma smiled. "I'll even fix you a cup of tea."

Jess was not used to being told what to do, but she didn't argue. She wondered what Cal had been doing the last few days. What did one do during this sort of weather? Kansas farms were shut down for the winter months. Once the winter wheat was harvested, everything slowed down. Cal seemed to keep busy here in this forsaken part of eastern Oregon. Jess closed her eyes and thought back to the last time she'd been part of a loving family. The memories brought some solace.

Jess remembered the hot, spiced tea brewing on the back of the stove when her father stomped in from outside. He'd been repairing the barn when the weather allowed, and he looked tired and out of sorts; but when he smelled the cinnamon, a smile crossed his face.

"Are we having a tea party?" he asked her mother, taking off his work boots. "Would some of those good cookies you made yesterday be left?"

Jess's mother turned from the stove and smiled. "You know I always set some aside for you. Wouldn't be right not to."

Her father strolled over and kissed his wife on the cheek. Jess smiled at the scene. She had never tired of seeing her parents together. They were a team. They loved each other, and it showed. They tried so hard to understand the wayward, stubborn Abigail, but Jess gave them no trouble. She hoped that someday she'd find a man who would love her as her father loved her mother and one she'd love back with fierce intensity.

Jess's mind went to Brady as she shoved her teacup away. He would be a good husband. He was hardworking, planned to expand his farm, and needed someone to take care of his house and share his bed; but Jess simply could not imagine being his wife, especially since he was not a believer. And as much as she admired him, as much as she knew he wanted basically the same things she did, she had no feelings, and those had to be present to make a marriage work. Or did they? Perhaps she was to trust, to give of herself, and the love would come later. Perhaps she should stop thinking of the cowboy who found Abby and comforted her in her last moments of life—the man who had tucked the newborn baby inside his coat and traveled the ten miles back to town. Cal was nothing like the man Jess hoped to marry. He was shorter than she was, and he had a stubborn streak; she'd noticed that right off. Yet she sensed a tiny glimmer deep inside her, a thought that wouldn't go away.

Each time she saw him, the feeling grew. She didn't want it to; it just happened.

"Miz Wilcox?"

She heard a voice at her elbow and turned to look up into the face of the man about whom she'd been daydreaming.

"Mr. Rutledge?"

This is so silly. I told him to call me Jess, just as he told me to call him Cal, and here we are being formal.

"I thought you might need a ride to the Downing cabin. I have a wagon out front."

"I—but how did you know I was thinking about that very thing?" She felt her cheeks heat up and pressed her fingertips to her face. "I so want to see Charlie again."

"I know." Cal's hat was in his hands, his gaze never leaving her face. It was that intense stare that unnerved her so, the look she couldn't get out of her mind.

"I thought you would never come." The minute the words were out of her mouth, she wanted to take them back. She sounded ungrateful after all he'd done. He seemed to ignore the remark and her flaming cheeks.

"Do you have warmer wraps than that?"

She wore a sky-blue dress, one of her best, though she wondered why she had brought such fine clothes. She had no place to wear a nice dress, nowhere to go.

"I have the coat Emma loaned me and gloves."

"And I have blankets—we don't have far, you know."

"I'll get my bonnet," Jess said.

Minutes later she sat in the wagon surrounded by two blankets, glad she'd worn her gloves. The snow still swirled, and she wondered when it was going to quit.

"Might be better by tomorrow," Cal said, looking over at her. "You never know, but I feel it in the air."

This man is uncanny. It's as if he knows what I'm thinking. How can he do that, Lord? She lifted her face skyward.

"When does the train come in again?"

The reins slacked a bit, but Cal stared straight ahead. "Friday. Always comes on Friday."

Jess nodded. She looked at his profile and wondered with a sudden fierce longing what it would be like to touch him. She looked the other way before answering. "I can't go this week."

"You *can't*?"

"There are two reasons," Jess said. "I don't think I should take Charlie from the only mother he knows right now, and I can't leave until I've visited Abby's grave."

Cal nodded but didn't look in her direction. "Tomorrow might be the day for the trip. Should know for certain by daybreak."

"I do hope it's possible."

"Yep."

"Do you suppose—" Jess touched his arm and felt a sudden tremor. "I would like to take some tea to the Downings. And perhaps some other food."

Cal slowed Dover's pace. "I think that's a right good idea. They don't have much."

"I could tell, and I drank the last of the tea yesterday."

Cal pulled up in front of the general store, hitched the reins to the post, then turned, holding out his hand to help Jess. "I'll come in with you."

"I can manage by myself," she said. "I mean, getting the groceries and all."

Cal's bushy eyebrows lifted. "Are you always this stubborn?"

"Stubborn? But I'm not. I just don't want to trouble you. It's kind enough of you to take me here—"

"I'll wait with Dover."

❧

Cal watched as Jess strode toward the door. She was elegant, far too fancy for these parts, and he saw a couple of men leering at her. It wasn't safe to travel alone, nor was it safe to be unaccompanied when shopping. He didn't think she understood that, but if he said anything, she'd scoff at him.

He didn't like thinking of her, the way she looked in that gorgeous blue dress—the same color his Millie preferred. And that bonnet that tried to stifle her curls, but the curls had a mind of their own. He didn't know why he thought of her again; no two people could be less matched. Yet something about her spoke to his hungry heart.

Silly old man, Cal chided himself. Not that he was old. He wasn't even thirty yet. But sometimes he felt old. Old and tired. And other times—like when he was around Miss Jessida Wilcox, he felt lighthearted and full of energy. *Silly,* he repeated. *Might as well smile at the storekeeper's daughter. She's more like you and smiles at you as if she likes you.*

Cal hopped down from the wagon and stalked toward the door. He figured Jess might need help since she would probably buy more than she'd said.

Livvy was in the back, holding up a bolt of material for Jess to examine.

"Material? You're buying material?" he asked, walking up.

Jess turned, her face suddenly going red. "Well, yes. I noticed Mrs. Downing could use a new dress."

"She doesn't have a sewing machine."

"But everyone has a sewing machine."

"Not the Downings," Cal said.

Livvy sidled up to him and smiled. "Mr. Rutledge, I haven't seen you in a long while."

Cal stepped back. "Been busy. Lots of things going on." Cal sensed how the young woman felt about him; sometimes a man could tell these things, but he felt nothing when he met her steady gaze. Nothing like he felt when he looked at Jess.

"I'll take four yards of this, and if she doesn't have a sewing machine, I'll borrow Emma's at the boardinghouse."

Minutes later they were in the wagon—the back end now filled with food, material, and candy that Cal insisted on buying for the children.

A yowling sound filled the air as they pulled up in front of the cabin. A horse and buggy were there, and Cal wondered who it could be.

The door opened then, and an older man came out. Mr. Downing. Had he suddenly returned from his job out at the Bar West Ranch?

He tipped his hat when he saw Jess and Cal sitting in the wagon. Neither had moved. "Me and the missus had a little spat. Seems I'm not welcome when I've been a-drinkin'."

Cal said nothing, but Jess seized the opportunity. "We've brought some things for your family, Mr. Downing. I do hope that's all right."

He spat tobacco juice out onto a bare spot of the road. "Well, reckon Sarah will be happy, and I'm much obliged, though it ain't necessary. You're the baby's aunt, I suppose."

"Yes, I am." Jess held out her gloved hand. "I appreciate so much what your wife has done for Charlie."

Mr. Downing swayed as he went off down the street toward the saloon. He didn't appear to feel a need to respond to Jess's words.

Cal climbed down, helped Jess, then handed her one box while he grabbed the other. "Might as well go on in. Maybe the crying will stop then."

Sarah Downing's eyes grew round in her face when Cal and Jess carried in the two boxes of groceries. "What's this for?"

"You." Jess drew the bolt of fabric out of one bag. "Material for a dress."

Sarah said nothing but kept shaking her head. The little ones flocked into the room. They'd been around Cal long enough to know he meant no harm. They still didn't talk, but when he said, "Candy," and held up the sweet sticks of confection, they suddenly chattered.

"This is better than Christmas," Sarah said, holding the material to her ample bosom.

"Now I think we should have a cup of tea," Jess said, looking at the oldest girl.

"Yes, Mary, go put the kettle on."

The house was warmer today since the wind had died down. Jess took off her outer wrap and went to look in the cradle at Charlie. He lay on his back, his little fists clenched around his chubby face. It seemed he had grown in just the five days since she'd arrived in Pell's Valley. How much longer before she could take him home? She wanted to be sure he was able to make the long train ride, and she had to find milk to feed him.

"Tea and candy," Cal said. "Found some candy you might like, Miz Downing." He held up a chocolate bar. "Nothing fancy, but looks good to me."

The eldest boy, Henry, came into the room on that word. Chocolate was expensive, and Cal had told Jess earlier he wondered if the Downing family had ever had any.

"Charlie slept all night," Sarah said. "He's growin' fast."

"And we have you to thank."

Now why did I say "we"? Jess looked at Cal, wondering if he'd heard the "we."

She knew what the baby meant to Cal, but she couldn't stay here. It wasn't possible. What would she do? She'd never seen such a heathen place. No church building, no preacher coming through. Only a saloon, the general store, a livery stable, and a boardinghouse.

They soon left, and Cal mentioned the sky was clearing. "I think tomorrow we should make that trip."

six

" 'Spect we should be heading out." Cal had arrived at the boardinghouse as the sun rose, bathing the sky with pinks, reds, and oranges. "We're leaving early because we need as many daylight hours as we can get. It's ten miles and a good four-hour ride."

He thought of the discussion they'd had the evening before. He'd referred to it as an argument.

"Can't we take the wagon?" she'd asked.

"Too slow. We'd have to stay out there overnight with no chaperones. Besides, if you saw the condition of the only building on my land, you'd change your mind mighty quick!"

"I am not a horsewoman," Jess had said. "I have ridden, but I wonder if I can go that far."

"The only alternative is if you ride with me. You could ride in back—"

Jess's eyes widened. "Oh, no, I couldn't do that."

"It's the only choice. Either you ride—I can find a horse to borrow—or you ride with me. We'll have to stop more often though."

So it was settled. He knew of a horse at the stables, a gentle mare, and it could be ready for their trip.

Soon they were on their way. Jess wore the brown muslin and black boots with a touch of fur on them.

Cal shook his head when he'd come by to pick her up that morning. "You don't look like you're ready for a long horse-back ride."

Jess lifted her face and turned away. "This is the best I can do. Who would have thought I'd be riding out on the prairie—"

"Desert," Cal interrupted. "It's a desert here in Oregon, not a prairie."

"Desert," she said through gritted teeth. "I didn't bring old things."

Cal slid onto Dover and gave the reins a snap. "Bet you don't even own any old things." Jess's parents must have had money for such finery. He couldn't help feeling sorry for her with no family to speak of. She must be bereft, first losing her parents and then her little sister. But no one would ever know it by her strong manner.

"I have lots of old dresses," Jess said, lifting her chin. "I thought I'd be here a day at most and then Abby and I would head back home to Kansas."

"I'm sorry the conditions weren't as you wished."

"It isn't your fault—"

"Yep, you're right on that."

Jess sat up straighter in the saddle. "Are we going to see anything besides sagebrush?" she asked. "I mean, it's all the same. How can you raise anything here?"

"Cattle," Cal said. "Cattle do fine here. We have rangeland with good plants to eat. Even have a water hole on my land."

"It's dreadful," Jess said.

"Well, it isn't where I'm fixing to build my house. I have a view of the Sourdough Mountains, and you never saw a prettier sunrise or sunset in that spot."

"What about trees and flowers?"

Cal paused, pulling on the reins. "Let's stop for a minute and stretch. You look tired."

"I'm afraid to get off the horse because I might not get back on."

"We'll just rest for a minute." Cal hopped down, looking around. "You haven't been here in the springtime when the sagebrush blooms. And there's a stand of English poplars— trees the fire didn't take."

"Fire?"

"Yeah. A fire burned down the house, but it miraculously stopped before hitting the shed—"

"You mean the shed where Abby died after giving birth to Charlie?"

"Yes, the shed was spared, such as it is."

"God provides," Jess said quietly. "If the shed had burned down, too, Abby would have had no shelter. Are we going to be there soon?"

Cal looked at the sky; the sun wasn't anywhere near the top of the sky, an indication noon was far off. And that was a good thing.

"We're halfway there, Miz Wilcox."

"Jess," she said. "Please call me Jess."

"I will when you call me Cal."

She tossed her head, making him think of Dover when he was protesting about something. "I admire you," she said.

Cal stared in disbelief. "Admire me?"

"For being strong and wanting to help and being there for Abby. For bringing Charlie back to town and finding Sarah to nurse him—"

"Whoa. Do you think I could have left a baby alone to be eaten by coyotes or wolves?"

"Of course not."

"I did what anyone would have. And we were lucky Sarah was just weaning her baby."

Jess took a deep breath. "There is a fresh smell to the air. I like that."

"Oh, finally found something you like about the desert?"

"Yes." Jess smiled. She hesitated. "What is your biggest wish right now?"

My biggest wish? What a laugh. If I'd had control of things, Millie would be alive. I'd be back in Montana watching my son take his first steps.

"You tell me," Cal said. "It's your idea, after all."

Jess took a deep breath, loosening the ties on her bonnet as the sun finally warmed the earth. "I always wanted to teach school, and perhaps one day I'll marry, have a family."

"Why can't you teach school?"

Jess shrugged. "After my parents died, I had the farm to handle and Abby. I pushed my dreams aside."

"And now?"

"Now I have Charlie to think about."

"And Charlie needs a father, so you'll go back to Kansas and marry your childhood sweetheart."

Jess stiffened. "I could marry the man next door, but I don't think I will."

"Why not?"

"Because I think of him as a brother, and one can't marry one's brother."

Cal felt something tug deep inside his heart. *She doesn't love anyone in Kansas. Perhaps I could convince her to stay here.*

"I think you should get your teaching certificate. Teach if that's important to you."

She didn't acknowledge Cal's suggestion but pointed at him. "Okay. Your turn."

"My wish now is to make this ranch thrive, to build my house and fill it with squalling babies and a wife who loves the area as much as I do."

"What about a wife who loves you?"

Cal got a faraway look in his eyes. "Had that once and don't think it can happen twice in a lifetime. The Lord giveth, and He taketh away. I'm wanting Him to give again, but only He has the answer."

❧

Jess let the words sink in. Cal was a deep thinker. She had not known that about him. He was worthy of love, and surely God had someone in mind. If only she liked Oregon better. If only she could be that woman filling the house with children. But she wasn't cut out for such a life, and Cal wasn't cut out for life in town. God had someone for her, just as He had someone for Cal. She believed it with every fiber in her.

They rode along in silence, and Jess wanted to talk; but Cal seemed to want to ride and not talk. She probably shouldn't have brought up the subject. How did one get over a spouse they'd lost? And a child, too? It had to be difficult. It was difficult enough trying to go on without her parents' love. And Abby, though capricious, had brought laughter into a room. Now Jess would never hear that sound again, and Charlie would never experience the love of his mother. Jess swallowed hard as the reality sank in. Yes, Charlie suffered the greatest loss here.

"It's up ahead," Cal said, breaking into her thoughts. "I can tell by the lay of the land, the way the trail bends suddenly. See the tops of those trees in the distance?"

"Yes, I do," Jess said. "We're almost there. I can hardly wait."

"Not almost there. It's at least an hour's drive away. Just wanted you to know we're getting close."

Jess began humming. She didn't expect Cal to join in, but his low voice picked up as they sang "She'll Be Comin' round the Mountain."

Jess laughed suddenly. Cal looked over, a wide smile beaming across his face. "I like it when you laugh."

She was about to comment when a gust of wind blew down from the north and she shuddered. "Don't tell me we're going to get snow."

"Nope. Not yet. It'll snow again tonight, but we'll make it back before the blizzard hits."

"How do you know?"

"Can tell by the feel of it."

Jess saw the shack then and realized they were almost there. Her heart beat fast as she followed Cal on the trail that had become narrower.

"The grave site is over yonder," he murmured, pointing.

Jess felt tears threaten at the thought of Abby being buried out here. What a place to come to, let alone die here.

Cal got off his horse and led Dover to the hitching post. He pointed to a small wooden cross and a pile of rocks. He turned and offered to help Jess down. She didn't want to rely on his help, but she was suddenly weary from the trip. She tried to stand when he put her down; but her legs buckled, and he caught her before she fell.

"Oh, my," she said, looking into his eyes, etched with worry. "I didn't know my legs would fail me."

He didn't look away, and she felt a sudden intensity and seriousness in Cal's glance.

"I'm fine now," she said, pulling away from his arms, his touch that made her insides come alive. *I can't let this be. I'm misinterpreting his look, but those eyes, oh, those eyes.*

❧

Visibly shaken, Cal walked over to the small grave, remembering how he'd held the young girl close for a moment, smoothed the hair back from her face, then set her down on the dirt floor of the desert. He'd had to get her buried fast and hurry back to town with the baby.

"It's a nice grave," Jess said. "Abby would have approved. I like the cross and what it stands for. She also would have liked the rocks. She used to have a rock collection—"

Then Jess was on the ground, her dress billowing around her as she lowered her head and wept. Her tears turned into gut-wrenching sobs as she pounded the ground.

Cal didn't know what to do. Should he leave her alone? Let her suffer her agony in peace? Or should he at least offer his handkerchief, the clean one he'd put in his coat pocket that morning? He took off his hat and bowed down on the other side.

"Lord, You know the grief Jess feels now. I pray for comfort for her soul, for Your everlasting arms to hold her close."

Jess raised a tear-splotched face upward and breathed an amen to Cal's prayer. She then added her own. "God, You know my heart; You know my failings. Help me to overcome the bitterness I feel at Abby's death, and help me to be a good, strong mother to Charlie."

Cal left her alone as he walked over to the shed. Surely nothing was left behind, but he *had* to do something.

He found the spot where Abby had lain, where she'd breathed her last. Traces of dried blood showed someone had died there, just as someone had been born. He turned and walked out of the shed into the sunlight of the high-noon day.

Jess met his gaze and sighed. "It's all so strange. How did she get way out here by herself? You said you saw no horse or anything around."

"I think the horse ran off before Abby could tie him up."

Jess nodded. "She was in labor, too."

"We may never have the answer," Cal said, looking up into the sky. "It's time to head back. No point in staying any longer." He'd brought Jess here as he'd promised. She'd grieved as he also knew she'd do. Now they'd return to Pell's Valley, and life would go on as before. Jess heading back to Kansas with Charlie, and Cal waiting for spring and for his cattle to come. It would be a long, lonely winter.

❧

It began snowing as they reached the outskirts of Pell's Valley. Cal took a weary Jess back to the boardinghouse, saw her to the door, and tipped his hat as she turned and started to say something.

"Don't thank me," he said. "Pleasure was all mine. Now get inside and get some food inside you. Maybe a cup of hot tea will help."

Cal led Dover and the mare back to the stables and went into the saloon for a meal. It had been a long trek, but he had enjoyed Jess's presence, far more than he wanted to admit. She bothered him at times with her bossiness, but she'd seemed docile on the way back. She had a gentleness she seemed to try to hide, and he didn't know why.

The saloon was quiet, as it always was midweek. Cal was thankful the dining hall was separate from the part where the men drank. The food was passable, and since ol' Blade had started cooking, the fried chicken was the best Cal had ever eaten. The fried potatoes and baking powder biscuits were good, too, now that he thought about it.

"Where you been, cowboy? Do I know you?" The hostess, someone he had never seen, smiled as she touched Cal's shoulder.

"No, reckon you don't. I come here to eat and sleep." He emphasized the word *sleep*. "Nothing more." Cal turned his back. It wasn't like him to be rude, but he didn't want to talk to the woman. Jess was right. This town needed a church and a preacher. Maybe it was time for him to look into it.

❧

Jess couldn't wait to get to her room and out of the limp dress. She felt dirty, exhausted, and stiff. Her face was chapped from the never-ending wind. How did women stand it here? She poured water into a small basin and dipped a cloth into it. Jess patted her face, liking the cool feeling. After freshening up, she'd go downstairs, and maybe Emma would fix her something to eat. She felt weak from hunger, and the emotional toll had drained her; but she was glad she'd gone. She couldn't begin to imagine what Abby had gone through, and all alone with no one to hold her hand and offer her comfort.

Cal's face came to mind, and Jess sank back on the feather bed, wishing she wouldn't think of him so often. He had his life here, and she had her life and home in Kansas. He adored Charlie, just as Jess did. Charlie reminded her of Abby when she was a baby with the dark, dark eyes, the thatch of dark curls.

She opened the small bag Cal had given her and took out the packet of letters. She had already read them but wanted to read them again. She reread the last one, visualizing her sister as she wrote it.

> *Jess, it's time to do some explaining, but I don't know where to begin.*
>
> *Life here is not what I had envisioned. I so long for the green, green grass in the yard of our home in Kansas. The roses Mama grew and took such good care of. I think of Papa and his hearty laugh. And you who only loved me and wanted what was best for me. Why didn't I listen? Now here I am, more than a thousand miles away and no way to get home.*
>
> *If something should happen to me, I want you to have all my earthly possessions, and I mean* all.

Abby had underlined the word, and Jess wondered now if Abby had been afraid to tell her she was with child. She probably figured her big sister would scold and say, "See—what did I tell you?"

Tears slipped down Jess's cheeks as she thought of the young girl writing the letter. She sounded so frightened and alone, and Jess wished she had some answers. Would she ever know what happened?

Jess held the small golden cross to her cheek, remembering the Christmas Abby received it—the year before Grandma Wilcox died. Abby had treasured the cross and worn it every day.

The gold button came from Grandfather Wilcox's army uniform. He'd fought in the War of Rebellion, between the states. "Was the most handsome man I'd ever laid my eyes on," Grandmother said. "And when he asked for my hand, I thought I was dreaming."

Jess put everything back in the satchel, thankful she had this much of Abby. A tap at the door made her jump.

"Miss Wilcox, I wondered if you were all right. Could I get you something to eat or drink?"

"Thanks, Emma. I'll be down soon."

"I'll put the kettle on," Emma said. "We have leftover roast with a bit of gravy and a few potatoes."

"That sounds wonderful."

Jess slipped into the blue dress she had worn her second day here. She patted her hair into place. Emma was nice; Jess had most of the comforts of home, but it could never be home. No place could be like her home. And with that, she thought of Cal as she headed down the stairs.

seven

Cal wasn't sure why he decided to go back to the boarding-house. He had no intentions of doing so, but somehow after supper and two cups of coffee, he could think only of seeing Jess again, remembering how she felt in his arms after getting off the horse and how she had crumpled over her sister's grave. His heart pounded now at the memory. She was taller, but did that matter? Not to him. Yet it was hopeless. Jess would head back to Kansas, probably on next Friday's train. Why did he feel drawn to her? She was different from his Millie. Was he clinging to the memory of his late wife, wanting to find someone just like her? Yet he liked being with Jess. How could that be?

Cal paid for his meal and stepped out into a clear night. Dozen of stars twinkled in the dark sky. Snow fell, but the wind, ever present, had died down. It was a beautiful night—the kind for courting.

Courting? Nonsense! He stuck his hat on as he crossed the wooden plank sidewalk. Dover nickered softly when Cal entered the stable.

"Going back to the boardinghouse," he said to his horse.

The lights blazed from the windows of the wooden two-story boardinghouse. Emma always had a pot of coffee on and managed to find a plate of cookies to offer him.

He opened the door, and one of the guests smiled at him. "Come on in."

Cal nodded to the man. "I need to talk to Jessida Wilcox."

He heard a stir in the kitchen, and Emma entered the room. "Howdy, Cal. Just made a fresh pot, and I'm sure that's okay with you."

Cal hung his hat on the peg beside the door and nodded. "Just had coffee, but I can always find room for more."

"Why are you here after your long day of riding?" she asked, clearing the dishes from a table.

"Is Jess here?"

"And where else might she be?"

Cal grinned. "I suppose there aren't too many places she could be, all right. Just wonderin' if I could have a word with her."

"She's been upset, you know."

"Yep, I can imagine. The trip was hard, and after seeing her sister's grave, she sort of fell to pieces."

"Doesn't surprise me none."

"I thought if she wanted to, we could go see Charlie. Haven't seen him today. The snow I feared is beginning to fall, but the wind has died down. 'Spect we'll wake up to a lot on the ground though."

"I'll tell her you're here," Emma said. "You wait in the parlor with your coffee." She handed him a cup and saucer.

"Yep."

Cal had finished the coffee and wondered if Jess had seen enough of him when he heard her voice outside the door. He stood when she entered the room. "You look rested," he finally said.

What he wanted to say was, *You're so beautiful in that blue dress; it's all I can do to keep from taking you into my arms.*

"I'm giving that old brown dress to Sarah Downing, should she want it. I can't stand looking at it anymore."

"Yep, she's about your size," Cal said with a nod.

"And why are you here? Aren't you worried about the snow?"

Cal felt a grin coming on. "The weather's changed a bit, and it's not far—that is, if you want to go see Charlie."

Her cheeks went aflame at the thought of Charlie, and she reached out and touched his shoulder. "I would so very much like to see my nephew."

"Fine. I brought the wagon and blankets, same as you used before."

"That is thoughtful of you."

He helped her on with a long velvety-feeling coat. "I trust you had supper?"

"Oh, my, yes. You know Emma. She insisted I eat, and then I went back to my room. Earlier I read the letters, and—I'm so grateful you brought the satchel back with young Charlie."

"Was happy to."

The sky couldn't have been more glorious as they rode east. Cal had lots of things he wanted to say, questions to ask; but he was a slow and deliberate person, and the timing was wrong. He couldn't dare hope; yet hope took over his being as Dover trotted along at a steady gait. It was as if the tall, beautiful woman at his side were meant to be there.

A light lit up the small cabin, and Cal found himself taking time to hitch the horse, to talk to his animal. "Won't be long, fella." Dover needed the rest and comfort of the stable tonight. He had more than done his duty. Cal looked sideways back at Jess, still sitting in her seat, the blanket wrapped around her feet, her face looking beautiful in the bright moonlight. How he didn't want the night to end. How he wanted to speak his heart, but he knew his head must rule. Hearts got broken, and he couldn't afford to let that happen again. Not ever.

❧

Jess watched Cal as he spoke to his horse, waiting for him to come and help her down. If she descended on her own, it seemed to distress him. She looked at him again. Rugged. Muscular. Dependable. Kind. Generous. And loving to his horse. How many more good traits had she missed? *Watch out. Keep thinking this way, and you'll regret it. Your home is in Kansas, not in some isolated hick town like Pell's Valley. Look to your future.*

❧

Cal walked over and held up his hand to help her. Jess wore

gloves, but she felt the warmth through them. She hoped he didn't notice her hand trembling.

The door suddenly opened, and Henry, the oldest Downing boy, stuck his head out. "Are you a-coming in?"

"Yes," Cal said. "Is Charlie awake?"

The boy nodded. "Yessir! He just got fed, and his eyes are open, and he's being noisy-like."

The room was warm, and Sarah stood in the kitchen, her hand on the teakettle. "I knew you'd be a-coming by. Hadn't seen the young'un all day."

Jess leaned over the cradle and pulled him into her arms. "He's growing by the day," she murmured, holding him up to her cheek. *So soft you are. And I love you so much. Can I be a good mother to you? You need a pa, though, and the one you need is standing in this room, watching me and watching you. Yet it cannot be. It just cannot.*

જી

Cal strode over and looked at the small face. His heart pounded with the love he felt for the lad. And the same feeling extended to the woman holding him, though he could not let it be known. Not now. Perhaps never.

The door swung open, and Elias Downing entered. His voice filled the room, and Charlie jumped in Jess's arms.

"Oh, thought it was you two again." He lurched to the side. "Hey, looky here. My family don't need your charity! You hear me? I can provide for my own, so you jest take back that food!"

Cal met the drunken man's gaze. "The food is for your family because we appreciate what your wife is doing."

"She'd do it anyway, don't you know that?"

"Of course she would," Cal said, refusing to back down. "But we can show our thanks in that way. Please accept my apology if we offended you."

"Well, it wasn't needed."

"But, Pa—"

Mr. Downing's arm reached out and smacked his oldest son

across the mouth. Blood spurted, and Jess let out a small shriek as Charlie cried. The boy did nothing, but he grabbed a towel off the back of a kitchen chair and left the room.

"We'll take the food back," Jess said. "I never meant to cause a problem."

"Oh, what do I care if you bring in a little food?" He turned and slammed back out the door.

Sarah, never saying a word, pressed a cup of tea into Cal's hand and motioned to Jess to put the baby down and have her tea. But Jess's eyes, filling with tears, didn't move as she held the baby closer.

Cal watched the sleeping Charlie in Jess's arms. He looked so peaceful, though he'd been frightened by all the noise moments earlier.

"I think we should be heading out."

Jess laid Charlie back in the cradle, covering him with the woolly blanket Cal had bought.

"I worry for Charlie's safety," Jess said once they were on the road heading back to the boardinghouse.

"I asked around about Elias Downing. He's never hit the girls, his wife, or the baby. He has it in for the oldest son; sometimes men are like that with their boys. Want them to be tough, rough, and ready."

"Ready? Ready for what?"

Cal lifted the reins, and Dover slowed. "Ready to be a man. At least I think that's what it's all about."

"There was no excuse for that."

"I agree."

"Why didn't you say something?"

Cal sighed. "Apparently you've never been around a man who is liquored up."

"No, I can't say I have."

"You don't mess with them. It's amazing the strength they have when they have a mind to. He could have laid me flat and broken every dish in the cupboard."

"Why, that poor family!"

"He comes home and lays his head on the pillow each night. Sarah loves him, I'm sure."

Jess shivered, and Cal leaned over, pulling the blanket up around her shoulders. Surprisingly, no wind was blowing, and snow was gently falling. Jess's bonnet had sprinklings of snow, and he leaned over and brushed off some of it. "We'll get a lot of snow before morning."

"I'm so glad we went to Abby's grave when we did."

"Yep, it was a good day to go."

Cal's hat was covered with the white stuff. He took it off and shook it.

"Things are rough here," Jess said. "I can't imagine living like Sarah Downing."

"She's an exception. Most women don't have a drunk for a husband."

"Why does he drink like that?"

"I don't rightly know."

Cal pulled up in front of the boardinghouse. Only one small light glimmered from the kitchen area. Cowboys lived a bare existence. People didn't comprehend how lonely it was. No, Jess wasn't meant for this rough life. Her home was in Kansas, not on some isolated ranch in the middle of nowhere. When Cal saw Jess to the door minutes later, she stopped and asked him about a Christmas Eve service.

"Christmas Eve service?"

"Christmas *is* almost here, you know."

Cal nodded. "I've ordered oranges to give away, stick candy for the kids, and something special for Sarah Downing."

Jess stepped inside and motioned for Cal to come in. "Just for a moment," she said. "I think it's kind of you to buy oranges and candy for everyone, but what we really need is a service where we can sing and worship God. Maybe even have a play." Her eyes sparkled. "And a Christmas tree is a must."

Cal leaned against the door, his mind whirling back to

Christmases of his boyhood. His mother—God rest her soul—had always made Christmas special. They had a tree, but it was the Christmas Eve church service that meant so much to him. The reading of the story in the Gospel of Luke, singing "The First Noel" and other special carols. All of that was possible here, but not the tree. In Montana they chopped a tree from the mountains, carrying it for miles back to the house. But Pell's Valley had so few trees.

"I think," Jess went on, "Emma will let me use the kitchen to bake cookies, and maybe we could have some punch for after the singing and Scripture."

"But where would we have it? We don't have a church, and nobody's house is large enough."

"We certainly can't have it out in the open," Jess said.

"The only place I can think of is the storage room at the back of the general store," Cal said. "It's the perfect spot—probably won't have many people, you know."

Jess lifted her chin. "I think you're wrong, Mr. Rutledge. I think we'll have the whole town involved."

On that note Cal bid her good night and left into the whitening world, his hopes soaring again. Jess was staying until Christmas. Otherwise, why would she be thinking about a Christmas Eve service?

He whistled all the way home, thinking good thoughts and talking to Dover. "You know, I'm even looking forward to getting up each morning now. What do you think of that?"

Dover tossed his head as if in answer.

eight

Snow blew fiercely from the north the following morning. Cal ate his usual breakfast of ham and eggs and drank two cups of coffee. He put on his warmest coat, stocking cap, and heavy gloves, then went out to hitch the wagon. The train would arrive soon, and he hoped the oranges and candy would be in. After giving Dover his oats, he headed to the general store. Livvy was at the counter and smiled when he sauntered in.

"Mornin', Cal!" She looked at him expectantly.

"How you doing, Livvy?" he finally asked.

"Getting ready for Christmas, about as ready as we'll ever be, I guess."

"You know"—Cal removed his cap—"I need to talk to your pa about using that back room where he keeps everything. It's good-sized, and Jess—that is, Miz Wilcox—says we need to have a Christmas Eve service."

Livvy looked surprised, then smiled again. "Why, I think that's a great idea. We can't get a preacher here though."

Cal laughed. "I know, but we can have singing and someone read the Christmas story from Luke. I could say a prayer. Miz Wilcox wants a tree, but we can't get one in these here parts."

"Guess sagebrush will have to do," Livvy offered. "We can always string popcorn, and I think Pa got in some red paper. We could make those chains like we did in school back in Indiana where I used to go."

Cal had never heard Livvy talk so much.

"That sounds right good. Maybe you could help the Downing children make them."

"Those young'uns? They're afraid of their own shadow. Besides, they're so dirty."

67

Cal thought of the soap Jess had purchased, sure she had noticed the same thing. Maybe they would have all taken a bath by now.

"Anyway," Livvy said, "I think you and I could make enough to decorate a squatty ol' sagebrush."

"Yep, I reckon you're right."

Sure can't be wasting my time on making chains or decorating sagebrush for Christmas when my cattle come in. I'll be busy with them and then building a house to live in. But for now I guess it wouldn't hurt to work on the decorations.

"Come, I'll show you what we have in the way of Christmas stuff."

A box of glass balls—red, green, and gold—with some red paper, a jar of paste, and a pair of scissors were in the back room of the store. "A gold ball can go on the top of our tree." Livvy looked at Cal expectantly.

"You know my ma always made a big thing of Christmas. We baked cookies for days and made the house all pretty, but the night the tree was brought in—" Her voice broke.

"What happened to your ma?"

Livvy dabbed at her cheeks with a hanky. "Ma died two years ago in September."

"I'm sorry."

Cal wanted to put his arm around her but was afraid it would be construed the wrong way. "I'd say you're ready for a party then."

"Oh, yes, I am."

The sound of the train whistle in the distance saved him from more conversation—something he wasn't good at anyway.

"Do you have supplies coming in on the train?" Livvy asked.

Cal paused. "Yep, sure do."

"And what might that be?" Her brown eyes were soft and warm. Cal looked away.

"Oranges," he said.

"Oranges?"

"Yes, for the Downings and possibly others—especially if we have the Christmas party."

Then Cal remembered he wanted to look at the jewelry case.

"Do you have any cameo necklaces?"

"You mean you're aiming to give a lady a necklace?"

Cal nodded. "That is, if you think it'd be okay to give a lady a necklace if you hardly know her."

Livvy's expression crumpled, but only for a moment. "I, for one, would be delighted to receive a necklace, and I can't imagine any woman who would not. Of course, it depends on who's doing the giving."

"Tell you what. I'll decide later. See you after I unload everything."

Two shorter toots followed the long toot, and by the time the train finally arrived, a lot of people had gathered at the platform. Some were there to meet family, while others were retrieving supplies.

Three passengers got off. Cal recognized two of the Stubblefield brothers, but he didn't know the tall man in the long, stylish overcoat and brown bowler hat.

The stranger grabbed a valise and stepped onto the platform. His highly polished wingtip shoes were not the normal footwear for the town.

Cal wondered, before the man spoke, if he could possibly be the Brady whom Jess had mentioned. Who else would be coming to Pell's Valley? But he thought she'd said he was a farmer. This guy didn't look like the farmers he knew. He was more the lawyer type, and his glance around town showed disdain just as Jess had shown when she arrived. Could that have been only a week ago?

"Excuse me, sir." He took off his hat. "I've come from Kansas—name is Brady Hollingsworth, and I'm looking for a Miss Jessida Wilcox. I don't suppose you know her?"

Cal stepped back and waved at the conductor and the young boy who had come to help unload the boxcars.

"It so happens I do know Miz Jess Wilcox, and I can tell you where she's staying."

"And you're—?"

"Cal Rutledge."

"I assume you live here?"

"That I do."

"And you've met my fiancée?"

Fiancée? Did I hear right? Jess never said anything about a fiancé. And I sure never noticed a ring. Wouldn't she be wearing an engagement ring? Yet a man doesn't travel this far to see someone unless he's in love with her. Not that it was a surprising fact. *Jess is maddening, but she is also beautiful and loving.*

"Yes, I've met Jess and yesterday took her out to my ranch—"

"I beg your pardon. Took her to your ranch? And where might that be?"

"About ten miles south of here."

"Do you know Abigail, too?"

"I did."

"Did?"

"Yes, we met under most unusual circumstances. Now if you'll excuse me, I have supplies to take off the train."

"But where is Jess?"

"Clear at the end of this road—you'll find an old two-story house, the biggest one around. I expect she's enjoying a second cup of tea about now. I was going to go get her soon to take her to see Charlie."

"Charlie?" Brady looked more puzzled than ever now as he shook his head. "Who is Charlie?"

"You'll find out when you talk to Jess. It isn't a long walk."

"But isn't there a wagon to take me there?"

"Afraid not. Unless you want to wait for me to unload my boxes."

Brady looked disgruntled. "No, I can walk. It doesn't look far."

That's what you think. Distances are deceiving in this flat country.

Cal found a crate with his name on it. He could see the oranges through the slats. The other was probably the scarf for Sarah and the books and toys he had ordered. He could hardly wait to see the children's faces. He wondered what Jess would do when she saw Brady. He wished he could be there to see her startled expression. Would she be happy? Of course she would be glad to see someone from home. He looked like her type. A bit sophisticated, intelligent, and—he stopped there. Though Cal was fond of Jess, Brady didn't seem likable, and his heart felt heavy. This could be the man who would be Charlie's father. And somehow he could not imagine Brady Hollingsworth being excited about that prospect. He'd see Jess later when she made her visit to see Charlie. He guessed he'd have his answer then.

Cal hoisted the box onto his shoulder and headed for the store. Since they were probably going to use the back room, he saw no point in taking these to his room over the saloon. But he was distracted by Mr. Hollingsworth trudging down the rutted dirt road. Jess had not said anything about anyone arriving from Kansas. Surely it would have come up on their long journey yesterday as they headed out to the grave site. This cemented the fact that Jess would be leaving with Charlie soon, and the empty feeling hit him again.

Cal hauled the other boxes of supplies into the store. He might as well help Jack Preston, Livvy's father, as much as possible. It was the least he could do. Livvy flew around like an excited child with all the packages to be opened.

"I spoke to my father about Christmas," she said.

"Already?"

"Well, sure. I knew it was important to you."

Was important. With Jess's fiancé arriving, I doubt she'll care about any Christmas service.

Cal was brought back to the present by the tugging on his

arm. He met Livvy's gaze. "And what did he say?"

"He wasn't too keen on it but said if you didn't mind moving things around, he could roust up enough chairs for about a dozen people."

"That should be fine," Cal said, estimating that many adults might come. The children could sit on the floor. "Thanks, Livvy, for asking. Now I better get busy."

Cal didn't want to say that maybe there might not be a Christmas party after all, though Jess couldn't leave before Christmas anyway. He would still have a party for the townspeople. He didn't want to disappoint Livvy, and he had promised to help with the decorations. Maybe Jess wouldn't sing; but he could still read the Scripture, and they could use Charlie as the infant Jesus. It'd be easy to find a Mary and Joseph. The whole idea seemed more appealing by the minute.

Jack Preston came around the corner as Cal unloaded the last pickle barrel.

"Say, Cal, I've been thinking about that room. Too much stuff in there to move, and I don't think it's a good idea."

"Do you have any other suggestions?"

"The saloon?"

"I imagine they'd not be too happy about us taking over to celebrate Christ's birth." Cal shook his head. "I don't mind moving things."

"I'm not a religious man."

"It doesn't matter," Cal said. Jack towered over him as most men did. He was used to it. "We just want it for one evening, and you don't have to come. We won't leave a mess, and I think a lot of people will be glad we're doing it."

"All right, but don't expect me to be a part of it. And I'm sure not handing out candy or anything."

"Don't expect you to. I bought candy."

The older man scowled. "Then nobody will buy it from me."

Cal shrugged. "I'm sure some will. As you said already, not everyone will come. I think we should put an announcement in the store window, if you don't mind."

It was finally settled, and because he had nothing else to do right then, Cal began stacking the boxes in one corner out of the way. The room would hold at least twenty people, and he doubted they'd have more than that. The Downings, Cal, and Jess—and now Brady—plus Livvy and probably Emma. He thought again about Jess and wondered if she'd want to lead the singing. If not, maybe Livvy could. But why didn't he feel a bit more excited? Why did his heart feel such a letdown?

nine

Jess washed her hair early that morning. It took so long for her thick hair to dry. She wrapped a towel around it, squeezing it until it was wet, then grabbed another towel.

Sometimes she pulled her hair back and tied it at the end with a silver clasp. It didn't matter how she fixed it, the curls sprang forth. Tight ringlets, a gift from her Grandmother Wilcox. Abby had always said she liked Jess's curls and wished she had curls, too. Jess felt the lump rise in her throat. It didn't seem possible that her baby sister was gone and she hadn't gotten to say good-bye. Hadn't been able to tell her how very much she loved her. But at least Abby had no more pain, no more heartache.

Jess wondered what it would be like to love a man the way Abby had loved Lenny Thorne. It was as if she had been overpowered and could think of nothing but him. How could she leave her home behind and go to a place she'd never seen? Jess knew the pioneers traveled by wagon train, following their dreams, but they went as families, not alone with someone they hardly knew. Abby, so lively and full of spunk, never had listened to reason though.

Would Jess ever feel that way about a man? She doubted it. She stared at her reflection in the mirror. High cheekbones. A wide mouth. But it was her eyes that were pretty, so Mama had always said. "Just like your pa's. Eyes that captured my heart, and I've not let go once."

Mama was like that. Some people just loved more whole-heartedly, she decided. Jess thought of Brady—it was the first time she'd had thoughts of him since coming to Pell's Valley. He was a good friend. He listened. He helped. And he loved her; she knew he did, but she could find no fluttering in her heart when she thought of him. The last time he'd touched her before she boarded the train, his glance had lingered, and she knew he wanted her to stop, turn, and come back down the steps to him. He had expected an embrace, she realized later, but she had turned away and waved.

Jess hoped Brady would find someone who loved him back. Several eligible women lived in the town near their farms.

Jess thought of Cal for what seemed like the tenth time that morning. She didn't want to think of him, but his face kept coming to mind. He had a kind soul and was someone to whom she felt she could entrust her life. She knew it from that first day and realized it even more after the trip to the grave site. And the prayer he had uttered tore at her. She would never forget the heartfelt words.

"Oh, Abby, Abby, it shouldn't have happened."

She turned away and pulled the chambray off the hanger. It was her second-best dress, and she felt like wearing it today. She'd go down and have a cup of tea and perhaps some breakfast, though she didn't feel like eating anything.

The dining room was quiet since no other boarders were present. Emma was banging pots and pans in the kitchen as usual. Jess heard a pounding at the front door, and Emma went to see who it was. "Hope it's someone from the train."

Jess's heart stopped when she saw the tall figure standing in the foyer. *Brady Hollingsworth. What is he doing here?*

Jess stepped back, but in seconds Brady saw her and swiftly crossed the room.

"Jess, I've missed you—I had to see you again." His mouth touched her cheek, and she felt the color rise.

"But it hasn't been that long, Brady. And look at you! I've never seen you in a suit before."

"I know. I bought it the day after you left, the day I knew I had to come. I wanted to look nice for you."

Jess looked away. "It wasn't necessary. But what are you doing here?"

"Aren't you glad to see me?"

Jess had never been good about lying, but she didn't have to lie. "Of course, Brady. One is always glad to see an old friend."

His face looked sullen. "You're not wearing the necklace I gave you."

Jess's cheeks flamed. She had forgotten about the package in the bottom of her trunk. She'd have to make some excuse. "I wanted to wait until Christmas to open it."

"Oh. That makes sense."

"But I'll open it now that you're here."

"How could you stay even one week in this place?" Brady asked. "I can't imagine anyone living here. The scenery is nothing but sagebrush, sagebrush, and more sagebrush. And hardly any buildings."

"I know it's a small town, but people are moving in."

And why am I defending Pell's Valley? Jess wondered.

"You're coming back to Kansas."

Jess stared at her folded hands. "I can't go. At least not yet."

"And why ever not? Get Abby to pack her things, and let's leave on the next train."

"It isn't that simple, Brady."

"And who is our visitor?" Emma asked, drying her hands with a towel. She had stayed in the background, as if trying to give Jess privacy. Now she smiled. "Do come in and sit down. I always have coffee on the stove and can find something to go with it."

Brady nodded. "I'd like that very much."

"Emma, this is Brady, a friend from Kansas, and Brady, this is only the best cook in the whole world."

Emma beamed. "Not that you've traveled that much, missy."

Brady took Jess's hand. "Now what's this about Abby?"

Jess opened her mouth, but the words wouldn't come.

"Aren't you going to tell me? Your staying on has something to do with Abby, doesn't it? The cowboy who told me where I could find you said I'd have to ask you."

"Cal? You saw Cal?" Even as she spoke his name, her heart did an upward swing.

"If you mean the short, bowlegged guy, yes."

"He's the one who found Abby and saved Charlie's life."

"Charlie? He mentioned a Charlie, too."

Emma came with cups, dessert plates, and the coffeepot. "I'm going back for the coffee cake."

She disappeared, and Brady pulled Jess to his chest, his hand touching her still damp hair. "Just take your time and tell me all about it."

Jess felt the sting of tears. *I've always been brave, strong, and determined. Why this show of emotion now?*

"Abby had a baby?" Brady asked.

Jess tried to stop her mouth from trembling. "She—Abby— died in childbirth. Her little boy lives because Cal took him to Mrs. Downing and she's been nursing him, keeping him alive."

"Did you see Abby, uh, before she died?"

"No. Only the grave site. We went yesterday."

"Oh. That cowboy mentioned something about taking you to his ranch."

"Yes. He buried Abby and said a prayer over her."

"I see."

Jess hoped her face didn't give away her feelings.

"But you're coming back home now with the baby—"

"I wouldn't go anywhere without Charlie. I love him so completely. He's all I have left of Abby; but he needs a mother's milk, and I need to stay here with him for a few more weeks."

Brady frowned. "That's understandable, I guess. Nothing's going on at the farm now anyway. We can plan on combining our property once you're home."

"Yes, I suppose we can." But her heart felt nothing.

❧

Cal wanted to stay away from the boardinghouse, but he had prepared the room for the service and couldn't wait to tell Jess. He had found the nicest, roundest, and best-shaped sagebrush to be decorated. Livvy had come in and exclaimed it was the prettiest sagebrush she'd ever seen.

"And we can make decorations tomorrow perhaps?"

"Yep, probably."

Cal stalked out of the room and out of the general store, looking west toward the boardinghouse. He had to see Jess and her fiancé together. He knew it would be painful, but sometimes one had to let things be as they were meant to be. Jess could never be his; he'd known it from the beginning. He was only fooling himself to think of it a second time. Yet the strong feeling began deep inside him every time he looked at her.

He stepped out into the windy, brisk morning. Without another thought he walked in that direction.

Minutes later Cal paused at the door, wondering what he would say. Should he offer to get his wagon and take them both over to see Charlie? Of course Brady would want to see the child he'd be helping Jess raise.

He knocked and opened the door. "Hello? Emma?"

Emma came and ushered him in. "If you're wanting to see Jess, she's in the parlor with that fancy gentleman friend from Kansas. But I suppose you already know that since you met the train."

"Yeah, we've met."

"And?"

"What's to know?"

"I think he's in love with her."

"Yep. I know he is."

"Well, come on in and sit." Emma put the coffee in front of Cal. "Here's the coffee cake they didn't eat." She put a generous slice on Cal's plate.

He pulled out a chair. "I probably shouldn't have come now."

"Oh, don't you worry about that. Eat up!"

Cal finished his second cup and stood, thinking he should leave. It looked as if Jess and Brady wouldn't be coming out anytime soon. Suddenly he heard shouting. The parlor door opened, and Brady stalked out, almost knocking over Cal.

"Oh, excuse me," he muttered. Then, seeing it was Cal, he narrowed his eyes. "Oh, it's you. What are you doing here?"

"I came to see—" He stopped when he saw Jess run out of the parlor.

"Brady—I didn't mean to—" At the sight of Cal, she turned and dashed up the stairs. Brady stomped outside, and Cal didn't know what to do.

"Just wait a minute," Emma said. "Jess will be back down soon."

"You think so?"

"Oh, yes, I know so."

"They had a lovers' spat," Cal said.

"No, I think it was quite the opposite."

Cal waited and had a third cup of coffee, and still Jess did not appear. Brady came back in.

"I have nowhere to go," he said. "I don't know anybody in this town." He saw Cal and lifted his eyebrows. "You still here?"

Cal nodded.

"You can stay here," Emma offered. "I have a room on the main floor left—it's small but comfy enough."

Brady removed his hat and sat down. "I guess I have no choice."

Cal stood. "I'd better get back to town."

"Just a minute," Brady said. "Exactly what has happened between you and Jess?"

Cal felt his face go hot. "Happened? Not a thing. I took her out on my land to show her where I buried her sister. I go over when she sees Charlie. Kinda got fond of the little feller."

"I intend to marry Jess," Brady said, his eyes narrowing again. "And I don't want any interference."

Interference? Cal thought. *That's a funny way to put it.*

"We're friends. Fear nothing more."

"That'd better be the truth." Brady looked toward the stairs, as if expecting Jess to appear suddenly. "I've loved her since we were kids, you hear? I've never looked at anyone else, and I intend to take her back to Kansas by whatever means necessary."

Cal grabbed his hat off the peg in the foyer, saying nothing. How could you argue with a man like that? Brady Hollingsworth wanted Jess, and he knew he would get her.

ten

The plans for the Christmas Eve service and party were finalized. When Cal asked Jess about it, she bristled. "Of course I want to do this, and I shall."

Cal and Livvy had made chains earlier. He'd felt like a schoolboy again. They made one long chain that wrapped around the sagebrush. It looked festive.

"We could also make streamers to put around the windows," Livvy suggested.

Cal nodded. "That's a good idea."

"Jess can be Mary," she said, "and Brady can be Joseph."

"I heard he doesn't want to take part."

"Then you can be Joseph," Livvy said. "You'd make a good one."

Cal shook his head. "I'm reading the Scripture. I can't do two things."

"But isn't Jess leading the singing?"

"That she is." Cal thought for a moment. "Do you want to be Mary? You have the right coloring for it."

Livvy's cheeks flushed as she nodded. "I'd be honored to be Jesus' mother."

"I think I'll ask Henry, the oldest Downing boy, to be Joseph."

"He won't do it—that family is so odd. He won't talk."

"Don't matter," Cal said. "Joseph was a quiet man, didn't have much to say. I think Henry will do it if I ask him."

They had no piano to keep them in tune for the carols, but that was okay.

❧

Jess woke on Christmas Eve with a sense of doom hanging

over her head. It shouldn't be that way, and she had to do something about it. She'd told Brady she wasn't going back to Kansas anytime soon, but he acted as if he hadn't heard. She had to tell him again. She wasn't sure when she would head back, but not next week. She didn't know why, but her heart was telling her not to go at all. *Not go? How ludicrous can that be? You have Brady who loves you dearly and shows it with every glance, every gesture. He bought a new suit and new shoes and came all this way to take you back, and you are ready to send him packing? Jessida, start using your head.*

She had opened his gift, and it made him happy when she decided to wear it. It was a golden cross, similar to Abby's broken one.

Jess drew back the curtains and gazed out on the snowy landscape. It was so flat here, but then so was Kansas. The only trees she'd seen were the poplars out on Cal's property. They stood like sentinels, as if guarding and shading Abby's grave. Could she not go because it meant leaving her sister to the wilds of Oregon? Or was it more than that?

She looked at the small drawing Abby had made when she was little. Abby with the laughing eyes, flying braids, and sometimes downright sassy tongue. How she missed her! But she'd left something behind, something more precious than pearls and rubies. And she sensed that Brady wasn't keen on being a father.

"I'll love the little boy," Brady had said last night when they discussed it.

"As your own?" Jess asked.

His expression was guarded for a long moment, and finally he said, "Of course, as my own."

But I didn't believe him then, and I don't believe him now.

One could tell how Cal felt. His face lit up whenever he was around Charlie. He loved the little boy. He'd be proud to be called his daddy.

But would he want me as his wife? Stop it, she admonished

herself. *Stop thinking that way. Cal loves Charlie, not you, and don't forget it.*

Jess reached for her Bible on the end table. She needed to bury herself in Scripture this morning, to hear words of wisdom from God. If she sent Brady on his way, she must be wholeheartedly sure it was the path to take. And if she stayed? What would she do? Teach school? What school? Where? The Downing children were the only ones in Pell's Valley. Would something happen to change that? And no church. How could she live in an isolated area where a preacher didn't pass through even once a month? Could she find something to do here? Could she make a difference? Why was she feeling missionary tendencies? Her maternal grandfather had been a Methodist circuit rider in Arkansas fifty years ago. Perhaps she had taken after him.

"Be still, and know that I am God."

Jess sat with her hands folded and closed her eyes. "Lord, You know I am rarely still, but help me to be still long enough to hear Your direction. Please guide my paths and help me know what I am to do. Amen."

She picked up an envelope from among Abby's belongings and pulled out a card. It was obviously something she had treasured.

Forgiveness is a necessary thing. "Forbearing one another, and forgiving one another, if any man have a quarrel against any: even as Christ forgave you, so also do ye."

Jess folded the card and placed it back in the envelope. She hadn't forgiven her little sister for running off with Lenny, nor could she forgive him. Not ever. She resented the fact that Abby had turned her back on Jess's advice. Was that why she was hurting so now? Was this what God was trying to tell her?

Jess closed her eyes and asked for forgiveness for holding in her feelings, for carrying a grudge. She had to get up and go on with life. Make the kind of world Abby would have loved. Rear her son with love and joy and watch him become a godly man.

Jess dressed quickly, pulled the quilt up over the stack of pillows, and hurried out the door. She had lots of things to do today. And time was wasting.

ᨂ

Sunday was a special day to have a Christmas Eve service. Jess made cutout sugar cookies that afternoon, and Cal had stopped by for a taste. They were in the kitchen, with Jess cleaning up the mess and Brady stacking the cooled cookies while Emma packed them.

"I have nothing to go home to, not if Jess is here," Cal overheard him saying to Emma.

Cal pulled out a chair, his eyes never looking anywhere else but at Jess's face. She had flour on the tip of her nose, her cheeks were rosy, and her voice sounded happy. The inner struggle of how he felt about this young woman began again, though every instinct, every fiber, warned him of the outcome.

Brady turned with a sudden frown, as if he could read Cal's expression. "I'm going to get ready for the party," he said, wiping his hands and leaving the room, but not before he touched Jess's shoulder. "We only have an hour to get over there."

Cal drank his coffee from the never-empty coffeepot on the stove and surveyed the kitchen. "Can I help clean up?" he offered to Emma.

"Oh, pshaw, never you mind, Cal. I'll have this place spiffy and clean and still make the celebration." Her eyes misted over. "I haven't been to a Christmas Eve service in such a long time. Won't know how to act."

Jess turned and hugged the short, wiry woman. "You'll act just fine, and remember you have the job of passing out cookies and punch." She turned to Cal. "Did Livvy make punch for tonight?"

Cal nodded. "Yep, she did. It's tea with apple and spices. Should be good."

"Then I guess I should get ready."

Cal stood and rubbed the speck of flour from her nose. Jess stepped aside, meeting his gaze for a moment before hurrying from the room.

"You look nice," Emma said, refilling his cup. "Never seen you in a tie."

Cal laughed. "Found this with my belongings. I have no idea where it came from." He fingered it. "At least it has red in it."

"It's quite fetching for a cowboy." Emma wiped off the table.

Cal didn't have a suit to wear. He'd worn one for Millie's funeral but had left it behind in Montana, figuring he'd never need it again. Now he wished he'd brought it. His dungarees were clean, and he wore a red plaid shirt, the closest thing he owned that seemed Christmasy. His worn boots were polished, but he still looked like a cowboy. Well, he *was* a cowboy through and through, and he guessed that had to be all right. A person couldn't change what he was, could he?

"You and Jess make a fine pair." It was as if Emma were reading his mind.

"Now don't go a-thinkin' something like that. You know she's going back to Kansas as soon as the next train comes in." *And I'll have four more days of seeing her.*

"I can tell what people are thinking. You may not know that about me, but these ol' eyes notice things. She's staying here. Trust me on this, Cal."

The wagon was ready, and twenty minutes later the four set out for the store.

"I sure wish we had more boarders to take in this most blessed of nights," Emma said.

Lanterns were coming from the direction of the Downing cabin. The children, usually mute, chatted and laughed. Henry carried the cradle that would be the manger. Jess went over to take the sleeping Charlie. Cal stood beside her, looking at the round cheeks, the dark hair framing his precious little face.

They trudged through the store to the back room. The

paper chains swagged from the windows, and the air smelled of sagebrush.

The sagebrush sat in the middle of the room, covered with the colored chains and stringed popcorn Livvy had made at the last minute. *Funny, how you don't smell sagebrush so much outside. But capture it and bring it into a small space, and it's pungent.*

"I love having a tree of any kind inside," Jess said. "It makes for a festive-looking room."

Brady grunted and shook his head. The room was small, and people filed in. Soon the chairs were gone, even with the little ones sitting on the floor. Sarah's children's faces were scrubbed clean, and Cal thought he caught the scent of the soap Jess had bought. Sarah Downing was alone, but no one had expected her husband to come. It was probably just as well.

Henry looked uncomfortable but smiled when Cal looked his way. Livvy wore a long blue shawl, and Charlie lay in the wooden cradle. So far he slept peacefully.

"We'll begin tonight with the singing of a few Christmas carols," Jess said, "but first perhaps Cal Rutledge would like to say a prayer."

Cal heard Brady Hollingsworth gasp. *Did he expect to be asked to offer a prayer?* Cal wasn't a preacher, but no one here was, and anyone could offer a prayer. Why hadn't Jess asked him ahead of time? He looked at her chin thrust out as their gazes met. He shuffled to his feet and made his way to the front of the room.

"Please bow your heads."

His mind panicked for a moment, and then the words flowed from him, words he didn't know were inside him.

"Our heavenly Father, on this special occasion when we gather to sing Your praises, may we remember the reason for this celebration. It's the celebration of the birth of the Christ child. And celebrate we will. We thank You for Your many blessings, and now may we please You with our words and songs."

Cal returned to his seat as Jess came back up. "I think you'll know most of the Christmas carols." She smiled that warm smile as she looked out over the gathering. "We'll start with 'The First Noel.'"

Surprisingly clear, strong voices rang out, and as Cal sang, warmth encompassed him. It had been too long since he'd sung on Christmas Eve, but even more his heart was filled with the presence of the Lord in a way he hadn't felt in an even longer time. It was as if He were in this very room, blessing the people. And the children, always quiet, looked animated, their eyes shining. Jess was a natural leader, and her voice rose above the others'.

It was time for the Christmas story, and Cal went back to the front and opened Millie's precious Bible. Luke, chapter two, was marked with her feathery handwriting. He motioned for Livvy and Henry to come and stand by Charlie, who represented the Christ child. He began reading, and it was as if he were transported back to that time.

"There were in the same country shepherds abiding in the field, keeping watch over their flock by night. . . ."

Cal was aware of someone coming in but didn't look up from the Bible. He paused now and then because he felt too choked up to continue. The silence of the room engulfed him as he finished the beautiful old story.

Jess thanked him when he'd finished and suggested they all stand and hold the hand of someone dear as they closed by singing "Silent Night."

"Keep in mind," she said softly, "that our celebration is to continue with gifts for each child and goodies to eat."

Silent night, holy night,
  All is calm; all is bright. . . .

Charlie woke when they sang the last verse. His lusty cry blended with the voices, and Cal walked over and lifted him out of the cradle.

If it weren't for this little guy, we wouldn't be here. Jess wouldn't be here, and I wouldn't be holding this child. Unto you is born this night a child. . . .

At the last moment Livvy's father, Jack, had said he'd be willing to help pass out the presents. He had slipped in when Cal started reading the Christmas story.

"Do you know I could hear the singing down the street?" Jack said. "And when I looked up, I saw the brightest star of all in the sky. It made me remember when I was a lad and we sang in church and I heard the Christmas story, just as I did tonight." His voice quavered.

This is the gruff storekeeper who never showed any emotion? Cal thought. *Oh, thank You, Lord.*

"What this town needs is a church, and I'm all for it, though I was against it before."

"Oh, Pa!" Livvy threw her arms around her father, her eyes shining.

The children loved the oranges and Jess's sugar cookies. Livvy had made popcorn balls. "It's my granny's recipe," she said. "I thought I had to give something."

Cal had no gift for Jess. He wished he had bought the cameo he'd looked at once. She wore a gold cross Emma said came from Brady.

"Mr. Rutledge," Sarah Downing stood in front of Cal, holding up the scarf. "I never had anything this beautiful. I thank you from the bottom of my heart."

"You're welcome, Sarah—I hope I may call you that."

"Oh, yes, please do."

"I could never repay you for what you've done for Charlie."

"It was my duty."

"No, not your duty."

"My blessing to give," she said.

The door opened, and Elias Downing staggered in. "Is my family here?" he roared.

The children, who had livened up a bit, shrank back and

stared at their father.

Jess stepped forward. "They are, Mr. Downing, and we're having a little party. Won't you join us?"

"I already been partyin'."

"Yes, I know, but we would love to have you come in for cookies and punch."

"Sarah, you comin'?"

Sarah motioned for the children, who flocked to her side. They had their oranges and the gifts from Cal.

"Thank you, thank you," she murmured as she and her brood went out into the dark, cold night.

"He could have let them stay a bit longer," Jess said.

Brady put an arm around her. "You can't change heathens, Jess. Surely you know that by now."

"I don't consider uneducated people heathens, Brady. That's where you and I differ."

Cal hadn't wanted to hear the conversation but was close enough to catch every word. Jess would return to Kansas, but was Brady the right man for her?

❧

Jess felt so blessed by the night's celebration. It was now midnight—Christmas Day. She and Brady sat in the parlor, recalling the beauty of the service. The train would come on Friday, and maybe she should be on it—but she wouldn't be. It was ridiculous, but she wanted to stay right here in Pell's Valley. The people had warmed her heart last night, and the shopkeeper's proclamation that a church building should be put up gave her the needed impetus.

She shivered, and Brady slipped an arm around her shoulder. "It was a wonderful celebration, Jess. Your voice is so beautiful. I'd forgotten how well you sing."

"Thank you, Brady." She turned and looked into his warm gaze.

"Do you like the necklace?"

Jess fingered the chain and nodded. "Yes, and thank you

again. Tonight was special, and I want to thank you for your support, your love, and—"

"And—?"

"Brady, I can't go back to Kansas with Charlie. Once I seriously considered saying yes to your proposal—your many proposals, I should add—but after the service my heart tells me my place is here."

"Jess, don't say that. Don't even think it." His hand reached for hers. "I can't bear to hear what I think you are going to say. I love you so much!"

"Brady, don't make this any harder."

"It doesn't need to be hard at all. Come with me on Friday. Come home where you belong, where a house is waiting, your parents' belongings, all the things you treasure—"

Jess shook her head. "But they're just *things*, Brady, possessions that can be replaced. My heart tells me to stay here where I feel needed. For the first time I feel needed."

"*I* need you. Isn't that enough?"

She avoided his gaze. "It almost may have been once, but not anymore. Brady—" Jess reached up and touched his face. "I'll sell you the farm. You've wanted it for years, and it's yours. Give me a fair price. I don't even want to dicker with you. I trust you."

"It's that bowlegged cowboy, isn't it?" His voice was harsh.

"Don't say that."

"Well, isn't it? Be truthful, Jess. That's one thing I could always count on—your honesty."

"And you can count on it now. It isn't Cal. It's several things."

"It's the cowboy," he repeated. He cursed and turned to leave, stopping in the doorway. "I'll be on the Friday train, Jess. Alone. But I have four days to try to talk some sense into you. Is it possible? I do hope so."

eleven

Cal didn't see Brady or Jess on Christmas Day. He stopped by to check on Charlie when he knew Jess wouldn't be there. He didn't want to see her with Brady, didn't want to think of the day when Jess and Charlie would walk out of his life.

Charlie recognized Cal's voice. Sarah commented on how the baby turned toward Cal when he entered the room.

"He doesn't like that other man," Sarah said with a shake of her head. "And Miss Jess, she acts different with him."

Sarah rarely talked, so Cal was surprised at her words. "How does she act different?" He had to know.

"Sad," Sarah said. "Not smiling as much."

Cal pondered this as he held the baby close. He'd never known his heart would feel so heavy.

❧

Cal left on Tuesday to ride out to the far south end of his land. He wanted to look over the property and knew a fence was down on the west side. It would be a long task, so he took his bedroll, provisions, and plenty of water. Jess would leave on Friday. He didn't want to see her off, but since he always met the train, it would be unusual for him not to appear at the station. Besides, how could he bear *not* telling Charlie good-bye?

The snow covered the ground in clumps as far as he could see. It seldom did so, but the wind had bitterly blown in. He hoped it would warm up by noon. It would be lonely spending most of his time on a ranch, but it was the only life he knew. Back in Montana he'd had his younger brother to do things with and in the earlier days his parents. His sister had moved away shortly after having her first child and now lived somewhere in Virginia.

Cal had gone to school as a boy but not beyond the tenth grade. He didn't see the point when all he wanted to do was herd cattle. It was what he knew, what he liked, and it could be a good life, even for a man alone. He thought of Livvy. She'd make someone a good wife, but he didn't think he was that someone.

It was slow going in the wagon but the only way to bring supplies. The ranch was his, and suddenly he burst forth with a song and felt better. Singing praises always made him feel better. How he'd loved the singing at the Christmas program. And things were changing for Pell's Valley. Jess was responsible. If she hadn't insisted on the Christmas Eve service, Jack Preston wouldn't have seen the need for a church. God had a way of touching hearts and pushing them in the right direction. How Cal wished He'd touched Jess's heart, making her see the importance of staying.

The wind stopped around noon, about the same time Cal reached his destination. He was close to Abby's grave site, and his heart quickened. Surely God had sent him out that day. He could have gone in a different direction and not found Abby at all. It would have killed him to come across a dead baby and the mother. But of course wolves or coyotes would have found the bodies and left little behind, only some hair, teeth and the clothes Abby had worn. Nothing of the baby but a small skeleton. He shuddered.

Cal worked through the afternoon, mending several yards of fence and feeling good about his work. It would be cold tonight in the shack, and he'd be alone. He had a lot to think about, and thoughts could be company.

He built a large fire that night. With his coffee in hand, he remembered a time in Montana when he and Tom had gone out to look for a lost calf. The nursing mother had come in for feed, but no calf. They'd found him, half-dead, and though they tried to warm him up, it was useless. It was the first time Cal had seen death close-up. He knew it wouldn't be the last.

His father tried to console them. "Boys, you done good. Sorry we didn't get to the little feller in time, but I guess it wasn't meant to be."

"But why did he have to die?" Cal persisted. "I can't think God would want the calf to die."

"It's the way nature works," his father continued. "Some calves are runts and not meant to live. It's a balance-type thing."

Cal had never forgotten the calf and the way he'd held it so close and prayed it would live.

He hadn't prayed for Abby; he knew she was drawing her last when he found her. But he prayed, oh, how he'd prayed for the baby born out in the middle of nowhere in the wilds of winter. Surely God would heed this prayer. And He had.

Cal finally slept. He wouldn't sleep long because he had to keep the fire going. He gave Dover his oats and hitched him under the eaves. He thought of sleeping in the shack but knew he couldn't with the memory. It was better to sleep out in the open. He'd be warm enough. If it snowed he'd feel the flakes on his nose, the only part that stuck out of the bedroll and covers.

A rising sun woke him early. The embers of the fire glowed as he added more brush and held his cold hands over the flame. He had to get a house built. Perhaps he should have thought of that first. Build a house. Buy cattle. Get a wife.

No. The last might not happen. Millie was still in his heart and soul, though he hadn't thought of her as much in the last few weeks. It was a fading memory, yet he could hear her laugh, see her ready smile, feel her arms entwined around his neck. It had kept him going these past ten months.

Cal began where he left off the day before. In another full day the entire fence would be repaired, and then he could head back into town. Tell Jess and Charlie good-bye. He so hoped he would grow up to be a fine lad. But why wouldn't he with Jess for a mother? If only Brady showed a bit more enthusiasm.

Dover whinnied, and he went over and unhitched him. "C'mon—we've got work to do. Oats come later."

Cal hooked up the wagon and headed out with the supplies, his heart suddenly heavy. Maybe he shouldn't be a rancher. Maybe he couldn't live the solitary life. Of course, once he got the cattle, he'd have ranch hands and the house to build, too, and that would keep him busy. He thought of something his mother had said. "Keeping busy makes you forget all that is wrong in your life."

Yes, keeping busy was the answer. And God was here, on his side. He could always talk to God, work things out, smooth things over. Yeah, it was time to head back to town.

꙰

Jess would stay with her decision. She'd searched her heart, thought about it almost every waking moment, and come back to the same thing. She wouldn't return to Kansas. Maybe one day, but not now. She was needed here, and she was one who needed to be needed. Brady said he loved her and wanted to marry her, but she wanted more. This flat, unattractive, scarred, dry, treeless land had nothing going for it. She hated it, but somehow it had grabbed her and was holding on tight. Or was she really staying for the cowboy with the twinkling eyes and the tender heart?

The Christmas Eve service and party had been beautiful and meaningful. Hungry souls who needed Christ in their lives had come. And with Livvy's father admitting they needed a church and donating a small plot of land, plus offering to start a building fund, Jess's hopes soared. They'd have their church, and she would help in any way she could. She could pound a nail along with the men, paint and scrub floors, whatever. And it didn't need to be fancy. They needed only four walls; frills could come later. With the sale of her Kansas farm, she'd have money to help pay for lumber. She remembered her church back in Kansas had recently purchased new hymnals. She'd ask them to send the old ones and maybe a few Bibles. A piano was in the future, as were pews. In the meantime they could sit on chairs from the storage room at the store. If only they could find a preacher!

"What are you doing?" Brady had walked up without Jess's hearing him. He looked at her scribbles on the paper and frowned. "Bibles? Hymnals? What's this about?" He sighed. "As if I didn't know."

"I'm staying," Jess said. "I told you, Brady."

"You're crazy! And I don't think you know what you're getting into. There's nothing here. A church isn't going to develop this town. How can you live in a place like this?" Brady crossed his arms and stared. "What about your prize roses—the ones your mother brought from Massachusetts? The house your father built? And what about me? What about us?"

Jess didn't like confrontations, and Brady seemed so good at them. "I'm not changing my mind."

"It's that cowboy! There's nothing like love to turn a woman's heart. And look what it got Abby. You'll be out there rustling cattle, cooking, cleaning, and taking care of a houseful of bawling brats like that Mrs. Downing. Jess"—he bent over and lifted her face to his—"that isn't you. It's not the Jessida Wilcox *I* know."

Jess pulled away. "People change, Brady. I know what I want. And if it's a houseful of 'brats' as you call them, then so be it. I feel God is leading me in this direction."

Brady stalked across the room and looked out at the barren road in front of the boardinghouse. "Yeah, that's right. You hear God talking to you. I'd all but forgotten that."

Brady's words cemented the feelings more than before. He had on more than one occasion chided her for her "insights" and doubted God really led people. He said people had to fend for themselves, and that's why they were given minds—for the power to think. She wondered how she had let things go on this long when they didn't share the same faith.

Jess stood now and straightened the blue chambray with

the white lace collar. The first thing she'd do was buy some muslin and make a few dresses that made her fit in. She'd get Livvy to help.

The thought of the storekeeper's daughter made her smile. The eager young woman with bright eyes and freshly scrubbed face couldn't hide her feelings about Cal. And that was fine. She wasn't staying because of Cal. His only tie to Jess was Charlie, and she'd never be second in a man's life. A man had to honor God first and love his wife second, and his family came third with the community next. Perhaps young Livvy was the right woman for Cal. Yet the thought made her feel empty inside.

"What time does the train get in?" Brady looked at his watch, then replaced it in his pocket.

"Nine thirty, I believe."

"Good! That means tomorrow at this time I'll be out of here, heading back to Kansas where I belong."

Before Jess could respond, he banged out of the door.

Jess closed her Bible, gathered her paper and pencil, and headed upstairs. She was glad Emma had not heard this exchange. Emma kept saying that Brady should pack up and go home. Jess knew Brady wasn't a quitter and thought she would change her mind. But she wouldn't. Her heart felt light as she wondered when Cal would be back in town. She missed seeing him and sensed that Charlie missed him even more.

Jess watched Brady from her upstairs window. The green-and-white gingham curtain fell back into place as she moved away. How long could she stay here at Emma's? With money from the sale of her farm, she could build a small house and still have enough money for the church furnishings. As soon as the church was built, she could have a Sunday school class. With Charlie close at hand, perhaps Sarah Downing could come, and she definitely hoped the Downing children would attend, though she doubted the oldest boy, Henry, would. He'd probably turn out like his father, but she didn't want to think that. Jess might hire Sarah to help in some way and pay her enough money to keep food on the table.

Jess knew Brady was an unhappy, angry man. He was used to getting his own way and was taking this hard. Yet once he was back in Kansas, once he sent the papers to make the sale legal, he'd be fine. He'd be back to his old self and would forget Jess. He had wooed her because of interest in her land; she'd always known that. Here again she was second in his life. She did not want to be second to any man!

Jess heard Emma arrive with the groceries and went down to help. She began peeling potatoes for stew.

"Are you really staying?" Emma asked.

Jess hesitated, a piece dangling from the knife. "Yes, I am. It's the best for Charlie, I'll feel closer to Abby, and, well, I want to see the church built."

Emma patted Jess's shoulder. "A person can change his mind, too. That's always an option."

"Yes, it is." Jess knew she'd made a good decision.

"If the supplies come in and word gets out, we could have a church building up in no time. Depends on how many hands are helping." Emma scraped diced onion off a plate into the soup pot. "Now getting a preacher to come is the real problem as I see it."

Jess finished the last potato and removed her apron. "You're right. So what might we do to change that?"

"I don't know. Guess we'd better think and pray about it—a whole lot."

They were setting the table when the door opened and Brady entered, his eyes glaring. Jess felt the tightness return to her shoulders. She'd hoped Brady would stay gone for a while; she didn't like being around him when he was angry.

"When's that cowboy coming back to town?"

Jess's heart lifted at the mention of Cal. "Are you talking about Cal Rutledge?"

"Who else?" Brady muttered as he turned and went down the hall to his room.

"Well, he's certainly cross," Emma said, "but don't you let it bother you. He'll be on the train tomorrow."

Gone tomorrow. It's good for Brady to return to Kansas. Yet I feel anxious. Here I am, two weeks in a new place, and I have to fall in love with the most unapproachable man of all!

twelve

The wagon was loaded with a shovel, a hammer, and the remaining bag of nails. It would be dark before Cal arrived back in Pell's Valley, and he felt impatient. He thought of Jess again, remembering the way her mouth turned up in that pretty smile and yet her eyes shot daggers when she was angry—the way they were warm and almost caressed you when she was happy. Her purposeful walk and how beautiful she was in that blue dress—the one with the white lace collar.

He'd never forget Christmas Eve, that night of enchantment—the sound of Jess's rich soprano voice as it filled that small room in the back of the general store. And everyone was as spellbound as he'd been. Then there was the way she watched him as he read the second chapter of Luke from Millie's Bible. No, he'd not forget Miss Jess Wilcox ten years down the road after she returned to Kansas. Some memories lasted a lifetime.

"Why don't you put this woman out of your thoughts?" he shouted in the wind. He thought he heard something once but knew it was only the wind playing tricks as it often did. Nobody was here. It was just him and his horse on his land, down in a hollow with the Sugarloaf Mountains in the distance.

Cal leaned over, giving Dover an affectionate swat. "Well, time to roll on back to town."

As he mounted his horse, he heard the sound again—someone yelling—and then horse's hooves galloping.

He pulled the reins close. "Easy, Dover. Seems we may be getting company."

Cal recognized the horseman as he came closer. They'd met only once, but one did not forget Lenny Thorne. Charlie's father—the man he'd tried to find. He took a deep breath, knowing Lenny brought trouble. He was that kind.

"Cal Rutledge, isn't it?"

"Yep, that's me."

The eyes glowered as he spat tobacco from the side of his mouth. He nudged his horse closer. Cal could tell the animal, wet from the hard ride, needed water.

"What can I do for you?"

Lenny swore. "Heard you helped deliver my son."

"Did no such thing. He was born when I found the woman in my shed here."

"Where is he?"

Cal stiffened, his knuckles tight on the reins. "Aren't you more curious about your wife?"

"I heard she died giving birth."

Cal nodded. "Yep, and I buried her over yonder. Said a prayer, too. But if you want to pay respects—"

Lenny stayed on his horse and removed his hat, wiping his brow with his shirtsleeve. "Ain't no respects to pay."

Shuddering, Cal looked away. He didn't have much use for such a man. No matter what happened between him and Abby, respect should be shown. "I think you need to," he said.

"You goin' to tell me where I can find my son, or do I have to go knocking on doors in Pell's Valley?" He spat more tobacco.

"Your wife's sister came—"

"Jess came all the way here from Kansas? What for?" For the first time he looked uncomfortable.

"Came to get her sister and now the baby—"

"It's my son, not hers," Lenny interrupted. "The rightful owner would be the father."

Owner? Cal felt anger rise to the surface. This man thought of a child as a possession, one that could be sold. Could this be what Abby had been running from? He'd heard tell of men selling their wives before, and he knew Lenny liked to gamble. He shuddered again before answering the man.

"I believe a child needs a mother, and Jess—that is, Miz Wilcox—wants to give her nephew a home. She's taking him to Kansas."

"Oh, no, she ain't!" Lenny jerked back on the reins, and the horse whinnied as it reared up.

"I tried to find you the day after she came to town."

"I been in Calyfornia. Been working my way back here. Arrived late last night, and the Stubblefields, where Abby worked, told me what happened."

"I'm not sure you have a claim here," Cal said, leaning forward. "You deserted your family, and Miz Abigail died out here all alone."

"A man has to make money to provide for his family."

"Yep. I know that."

The conversation was going nowhere. But Cal knew as well that the man before him was a thief and a scoundrel who would stop at nothing to get his son. He'd make things ugly for Jess, and what could Cal do? He couldn't see Charlie going to this man. He'd never be the sort of father a child needed. Selfish. Thinking only of himself. If he were any kind of person, he'd agree Jess was the best one to raise the boy.

"This here yore land?"

Cal nodded. "Bought it a month ago."

"You going to live out here?"

Cal wondered why the man wanted to know. What did it matter where he lived?

"I jest wanted to know. I'm going into Pell's Valley now, and I'll ask around until I find my boy. Boys belong with their fathers, not aunts. Abby would have wanted it that way." His face softened for a moment. "Besides, I'm changed now— different from when I was with Abby. Seen the light, as some say. Guess all that praying Abby did worked."

Is he changed? Somehow Cal didn't believe it. And would Abby want Lenny to have her son? If so, why had she written to her sister, asking her to come? Cal knew it was pointless to argue with this man. Lenny Thorne didn't care what happened to Charlie. All he wanted was a fight, and he was sure he'd get it. He also knew Jess would never give up Charlie without a struggle. And Cal would help. He owed the deceased mother that much. Even more he owed it to Charlie and to Jess.

"There's water over that incline—for your horse." Cal pointed. "I'm heading back now."

"Horse don't need water."

"It's a long ride back to town."

"Yeah, s'pose you're right." He led his horse to the small pond and waited while he drank.

"And your wife's grave is over by that small fence."

"Told you I don't believe in praying and such—"

Cal took a deep breath. "Thought you said you'd changed and all."

The younger man's eyes narrowed. "You already said a prayer—no need for me to say one."

"Whatever you say."

Lenny left, barreling north, and Cal urged Dover on. He wished he could get back to Pell's Valley before Lenny Thorne, but he knew it was impossible since he had the wagon. He hoped Lenny wouldn't make trouble when he arrived in town and also hoped nobody would tell him where Charlie was. Cal wanted to be there to ward off any trouble; his thoughts went to Jess and what this would do to her. Lenny would fight for his child because he liked to fight. Being the father, a judge could grant him custody. Cal had to do something, but what?

Cal followed the rising dust for a few yards, and then Lenny Thorne was out of sight. He could never have kept up with him, wagon or not. Not that he wanted to. He didn't like the man. He was unscrupulous beyond a doubt.

❧

Jess sat across from Brady for their last meal together. He'd barely spoken two words since his outburst earlier. She knew he had gone back to town and ordered liquor; she could smell it on him. How she hated the smell. He sat with that petulant look, moving his food around on his plate like a small child.

"Brady, I want to say—"

He shoved back his chair. "It doesn't matter now. You made your choice." He turned and stalked out the door.

After clearing the table and sitting in the parlor alone, Jess had a sudden feeling something was wrong. It had nothing to do with Brady, but someone else. Cal. Had he made it back to town today, or was he still out on his land repairing fences? Maybe it was Charlie. Could he be sick? She'd seen him that morning but had a sudden longing to see and hold him again. It was a long walk, but she could manage. She had to hurry; daylight was fading.

"You going somewhere?" Emma asked when Jess put on her warmer cloak.

"I want to see Charlie."

"It's late. Why don't you take my horse?"

"I'm more comfortable walking."

"It'll be dark before you get back," Emma pointed out. "Here—I'll hitch up the wagon and go with you."

"That isn't necessary, Emma."

"You never know when a storm could blow up. I'm coming with you."

One did not argue with Emma when she'd made up her mind.

As they approached the Downing cabin, Jess recognized a loud voice coming from inside. She froze. She'd heard it only once raised in anger but would know it anywhere. Lenny Thorne. He'd returned from who knew where and was standing at the Downing door yelling and cursing.

"It's my son, and I want him!"

Jess hopped down, lifting her skirts, and ran the rest of the way.

"Mrs. Downing, don't let him have Charlie!" she cried.

Lenny whirled and raised his fist. "So you are here. That dumb cowboy was right."

He's seen Cal? Cal sent him here? But how could he do such a thing? Jess's insides recoiled.

"How did you know your son was here?" Emma asked, puffing as she hurried up.

"Asked around. Wasn't hard."

"Cal told you," Jess said.

"What? That dumb cowboy? He wouldn't tell me a thing. I want my son, and I want him now! I'll take him if I have to burn the house down!"

"No, wait." Jess had to think fast. "There's a sane way to solve this. We'll find a judge and have a hearing to determine who will raise this little boy."

"He's my kid."

"He may well be. But you deserted Abby when she needed you, and she's dead now." Tears threatened, but she wouldn't give Lenny the satisfaction of seeing her cry. Emma slipped an arm around her shoulder.

"I left to find work. You can't fault a man for that!" Lenny took a step toward the door. Sarah shrank back, arms folded across her chest. Lenny pushed his way past her on the top step. A scuffling sounded as a gun barrel pointed out the door into Lenny's chest.

"Yore stoppin' right there."

Jess gasped at Henry standing with the rifle in hand. "No, wait!" she cried. "Don't shoot him."

"I ain't a-fixin' to unless he tries to come in. This here's my home, and I 'spect I have some say who comes in and who doesn't. When Pa's gone, I'm the man of the house."

"Now, Henry." Sarah's eyes were wide in her face.

Lenny stepped back, cursing again. "A man's got his rights. You'd better watch your back, because this ain't over. I'll return, and it might be in the middle of the night!" He spat and turned around, stopping in front of Jess. "Seems you have a way of poking your nose where it don't belong. You go get your judge or whatever, and we'll have this out."

"You aren't fit to raise a child!" Jess shot back.

"And of course you are with your highfalutin ways." He raised his fist, acting as if he might hit her, but stopped within an inch of her face. "I've done some real soul-searchin', and I'm a changed man. I may not look like it now, but I been ridin' all day. I will be a fit father for my son."

Jess trembled as Lenny stalked past her, mounted his horse, and galloped off in the direction of the saloon.

"Miz Wilcox, you come in now," Sarah said. "Charlie's awake and crying for you."

Jess and Emma entered the small house, and Jess went straight to the cradle. "Oh, my precious one! How can I let that awful man take you? He knows nothing about raising children. No, I can't do it. I'll fight this with every ounce of strength I have."

Emma patted her shoulder and agreed. "It's the only way, Jess."

Yet even if I do win, it's no guarantee Lenny won't be back later. O Lord, help!

Later in the quiet of her room at the boardinghouse, Jess said her prayers. God had to be on her side. Surely He knew Charlie was better off with her. But what might a judge say? Lenny had rights as the father, but the thought of him even holding Charlie terrified her. She had to find a way to prove she was the one most fit for raising the infant. But what would that be? Perhaps Cal had some ideas. And at the thought of Cal with his gentle ways and kind eyes, her love for him bubbled within, and she could hardly wait to see him. *But I can't tell him how I feel. Not now. Maybe never.*

She lay on the bed and watched the stars in the sky from the window; the sky that had comforted her since coming here now seemed dark and ominous.

thirteen

Cal arrived home exhausted. He heard loud noises coming from the bar as he made his way up the stairs to his rented room. During the week it was quiet, but cowboys came in on Thursdays and partied until Sunday. Jess was right. This town needed a church, and souls needed saving.

He woke up once in a sweat as he heard what he thought was Lenny Thorne's voice. So he *had* made it to town. Cal wondered if he'd found where his son was living. Maybe he was waiting for morning to begin his search. He knew what it would do to Jess and wished he could spare her the heartbreak. If only she'd left and returned to Kansas before this. But people like Lenny Thorne would follow someone, and of course he knew where Jess lived.

He visualized Jess now, holding the baby close, crooning to him in that soft voice, Charlie looking content. He needed a mother, and Jess was the perfect one. If only a judge would see it that way. With a man like Lenny, Jess would need the law on her side, and she may well have to take the matter to court. Cal wondered if a ruling would go against Jess because she was unmarried. The judge might think a child needed both a mother and father. But Lenny was not married, so it seemed to be a toss-up. He also wondered if they'd have to travel to the county seat for a hearing. He didn't think a judge would come to Pell's Valley. The town was growing, but for now it was just a speck on the map.

Cal rose before daybreak, took Dover, and rode to the boardinghouse. Jess wouldn't be up yet, but he knew Emma would have the coffeepot warming.

The light in the kitchen was burning. He smiled when he smelled the coffee.

"So you did get back." She poured a cup and sat across from him. "Jess isn't going to Kansas. Did you know that?"

Cal set his cup down, sloshing coffee on the table. "She isn't?"

"A lot has happened since you've been gone." And then she was telling him about Lenny and his threats.

"Yep, I saw Lenny, and I *heard* him at the saloon last night."

Brady walked into the dining room and stopped when he saw Cal at the table. "So the cowboy returns. Just in time, I might add."

Cal looked at his watch. "It's early, but I can take you to the train station."

Brady glowered. "I know you can't wait to get rid of me, but I have a ride, thank you."

Cal nodded. "Good." *He hates me and blames me for Jess staying. Guess I'd feel the same way.*

ᕯ

Jess awoke as the sun came over the horizon, streaking the sky with brilliant reds and pinks. Good thoughts flowed through her, even as she remembered the turmoil from the night before. She had prayed for strength, and God had given her peace.

She grabbed her everyday frock and pulled her hair back hastily. She had no time to take a leisurely bath. She had to go and see if Charlie was all right. Somehow she sensed that Henry had stood guard all night long. It might not be his baby brother, but she knew he felt a fierce loyalty.

Brady's suitcase was at the door, and he was putting his hat on when Jess came down the stairs. "I'm leaving, Jess. Are you going to at least give me a good-bye kiss?" His forlorn look was supposed to melt her heart and change her mind, but it was past that.

"You don't know what happened, do you?"

"No, perhaps not. Suppose you tell me."

"Charlie's father came to the Downings' last night. He threatened to take his son and might have succeeded if it hadn't been for the oldest boy holding a gun on him."

Brady shook his head. "See what you're getting into, Jess? Lenny is the father. The baby's rightful place is with him."

Jess's cheeks went hot. "Don't you remember how he treated Abby, how he acted when we first met him?"

"Maybe he's changed."

Jess nodded, her fingers clutching the sides of her dress. "Maybe so, but I sure didn't see any sign of it last night."

"Well, your cowboy returned and is waiting for you in the dining room. He'll make things right for you."

"He *isn't* my cowboy. Why do you keep inferring that?" Jess paused. "You said he's *here?*"

Brady shook his head. "Jess, you're so transparent. All one has to do is look at your face when he enters a room. Do you think I'm blind?"

Jess fought back sudden anger. "Cal's good with Charlie," was all she managed to say.

"I hope you come to your senses one day, and it'd better be soon." He paused at the door. "I'm not going to wait forever. Just want you to know that."

"Brady—"

"Save your words. Howard is taking me to the station. If you should change your mind, let me know. In the meantime I'll have the papers for the sale drawn up."

Jess watched Brady walk out of the boardinghouse. *Am I doing the right thing? Will I regret this decision? Brady is a good, honest man. And he loves me. But we don't agree on what's important. And I don't love him enough to marry him.* She sighed. *A chapter of my life is ending. I hope this is Your answer for me, Lord.*

&

Cal heard only part of the conversation in the foyer. He found Jess leaning against the door.

"I know about Lenny," he said. "He was at my place but wouldn't listen to reason."

"I heard," Jess said. She blew her nose. "I prayed you'd be back today."

"I thought you might be leaving on the train."

Jess shook her head. "No. I can't go now."

"Are you two going to come and have some scrambled eggs, or are you going to stand there all morning talking?" Emma wagged a spoon at them.

"Coming," Cal said.

"What's going to happen?" Jess asked, waiting as Cal pulled out her chair.

"You need to fight for custody."

"I probably don't have a chance."

"We don't know that."

"I wish we had a lawyer here in town."

"The county seat is a half day's drive away. I say you need to get over and file for a hearing."

Emma brought eggs, a platter of sliced ham, and a stack of her famous buttermilk pancakes. "Listen to Cal. He's right on this."

"In the meantime, from what you've told me about last night, I think Henry will stand guard over the young one."

"Oh, I pray he does."

"Lenny's not going to stay in town. He'll probably go back out and work at the Stubblefield ranch. Maybe see if they'll help him."

They made plans as they finished breakfast. He had many things he wanted to say to Jess, but the time wasn't right. The time would never be right, he figured. Why had God given him love for this woman? Why couldn't he have these feelings for Livvy? It would make things so much easier.

"I have to see the train off," Jess said, pushing back her chair, "in spite of what Brady said."

"That's wise," Emma said.

"I'll head on over to the Downings' after I drop you at the station," Cal added.

❦

Jess wanted to talk to Cal as they rode toward the train station, but the words didn't come. The thoughts in her heart had to stay there. Cal loved Charlie and would do anything for him. From what he'd told her, he thought she would be the best parent for the baby, and he also knew how she felt about Abby and how guilt haunted her. If she had Charlie, it would be like having a part of Abby with her again. The silence was comforting to her in a way.

❦

Cal wanted to assure Jess that things would work out, but he didn't know that. He wished he did. He also wanted to reach over and take her hand, but that would be presumptuous. If Jess won custody, nothing would keep her here—unless it was seeing the church built. But that wouldn't take long. No. He had no guarantee she would stay in Pell's Valley.

Brady stood at the platform alone. The train whistle sounded in the distance. Jess didn't wait for Cal to help her. She lifted her skirts, jumped down, and ran over to Brady. Usually Cal had something coming in on the train, but not this time. He heard Jess saying, "Brady, I want no hard feelings here."

"It's all right, Jess."

"Are you sure?"

"Yes." But his voice was flat.

Cal headed the wagon down the street. He hadn't seen Charlie for three days and was eager to hold the infant. He looked back at Jess once to see if she was hugging Brady, but the train rolled in, hiding them both.

The door of the Downing home opened before he knocked. Henry stood, rifle still in hand. "Oh, Mr. Rutledge, it's you."

"And you greet me with a rifle?"

"Coulda been that other guy," Sarah said. She was holding Charlie at her breast as she rocked back and forth.

"I heard there was a commotion last night."

"The father wants Charlie."

"And I couldn't just let him take him," Henry added.

"You're right. You did the right thing, son." Cal looked at what he could see of the baby's face. "I missed him while I was gone."

"He's been fine," Sarah said.

"I want him to stay here," Cal said, "if you can keep on feeding him until we get this settled."

"I figured as much."

Two of the younger girls came out and sat at Cal's feet. One had the book, the other the doll he'd bought as Christmas gifts. He smiled at them, and they smiled back.

"We'll have a hearing over in Vale at the courthouse. Make this all legal."

Sarah nodded.

The whistle sounded again, and Cal breathed a sigh of relief. Brady was gone, and Jess had stayed. Sarah handed the baby over, and Cal liked how Charlie felt in his arms. It felt right, the way it would have if his own son had lived.

He heard a tap on the door, and Jess entered the room. Cal felt hopeful when he saw Jess's face, as his strong emotions overpowered him. It was different from what he'd had with Millie; it had been good with Millie, but this was not the same. He had everything he wanted in life right here in this little room in a crude shack built in a town he hadn't known existed six weeks ago. When Jess smiled, it was a sign. He wasn't sure how or when, but it was as if God had just said, "Son, all you have to do is ask and you will receive."

Cal handed Charlie to Jess, their hands touching briefly. He met her steady gaze with a smile.

fourteen

Later that morning when Cal asked around for Lenny Thorne, nobody had seen him. Sheriff Wall was back in town. Lenny wouldn't cause any problems, or he'd be arrested. The sheriff had warned him after the last fight he'd had while playing cards at the saloon.

Cal stopped at the general store to find Jack behind the counter, where he usually saw Livvy.

"What can I get you?" Jack asked.

"I'm needing some baby things. That Charlie is outgrowing his nightshirts."

"Take a look on back—you know where they are."

After Cal paid for his purchases, Jack told him about the building crew.

"Part of the lumber's coming in on next week's train. I have six men lined up. How about you?"

Cal nodded. "Yep. I'll be there."

Jack shook his head. "You know, that Miz Wilcox is not only beautiful but a convincing woman. Makes me think of my dear departed wife. She would have talked me into moving the moon if it'd been humanly possible."

Cal felt a wrenching inside him. It hadn't occurred to him that someone else might be vying for Jess's attention. How silly he'd been. Of course men would pursue her. She *was* beautiful. A man would have to be blind not to notice.

"How about you?" Jack asked. "You going to be building your house soon?"

Cal grabbed the parcel of baby clothes. "Yep. Stuff coming in on the same train. I'm just waiting for spring for the cattle."

Cal walked back over to the Downings' and presented the

package to Sarah. "For Charlie here."

He felt Jess watching him, but for some unexplainable reason, he couldn't meet her gaze.

"I'm going to help set up the crew for the building of our church. It's to begin next Friday right after the train drops off the lumber."

"Oh!" Jess exclaimed. "To think we'll have a church soon. I can hardly wait."

"That we will." Cal stuck his hat back on and stepped back into the cold, late December air.

❧

True to his word, Brady sent papers for Jess to sign, and by mid-January she received the money for the sale of the farm. It came via the stagecoach from Vale. She also heard on that day that her old church in Kansas was happy to send a dozen hymnals and would include ten Bibles as well. Jess waved the letter in the air and ran into the store.

"I can pay my share for the lumber now," she told Jack Preston.

He looked puzzled. "You sure you still want to do this?"

"Oh, yes. I've never been in on the building of a church before. It's exactly what I want to do. How long will it take to build?"

"If we get all the lumber in and with everyone working, I'd say about five days."

"Five days!" Jess couldn't believe it. She thought of the months it had taken for the new church to be built back in Kansas.

"It'll be a plain building, ma'am," Jack said. "Nothing fancy for these here parts. If it was too fancy, nobody would come."

Jess felt her face flush as her hand tightened on her reticule. "I understand." She hesitated. "Thank you for donating the land for the church."

"You were right. We need a church here. Glad you pointed that out, Miz Wilcox. Now if we can only find a preacher. . ."

Jess had written another letter to her former church.

> *We are in desperate need of a preacher here in Pell's Valley, Oregon.*
> *It must be someone wanting to brave the wilds of this eastern Oregon*
> *town. It will be an adventure. And there are many souls to save and*
> *many yearning to hear the gospel preached again. And, I daresay,*
> *some have never heard about God's love.*

So far she'd received no reply to that request, but they had time. Once the building went up and they had a stove and the Bibles and hymnals, they would be ready for a preacher.

"The Lord provides for our every need," her mother had said more than once. "I see it every day in my life."

And so had Jess. Why else had she come to this unknown spot? Was it only because of Abby? For Abby's child? Or was she needed in a greater capacity? And perhaps needed by a lonely man who went out of his way to help others?

Jess drove the wagon back to the boardinghouse. It was time to help Emma with the noon meal. How glad she was for Emma's friendship and how grateful she was for her new life in Pell's Valley.

❧

January ended with a vengeance. Blizzard followed blizzard. All building was curtailed.

"May need to wait until spring," Jack said. "I've never seen a winter this hard."

Jess had sent for some reading books and decided to have a small class in the Downing cabin. Everyone but the new baby and Henry was eager to learn.

"I wish you could see Mary's face," Jess told Emma one evening over a cup of tea and a slice of her lemon cake.

"Reading opens up a whole new world," Emma said. "I wouldn't mind having some lessons myself."

"*You?*" Jess stared at the older woman. "You can't read?"

"I never went to school. My pa said he needed all the hands he could get on the farm, and that was that."

"But didn't your mother protest? And how about the school

authorities? Seems they would have come asking questions."

"Not in the little town where we lived."

Jess began with Emma that night, and she learned quickly. Jess sent for more books, knowing one day they'd have a library and the books could go in there. She was teaching, something she'd longed to do since she could remember.

☙

Cal approved wholeheartedly of her efforts. "Yep. Never seen Emma so excited. And what you're doing for the Downing children is good."

I felt as if something was going to happen the day you stepped off the train, even though you made me angry with your demands.

Jess's face turned pink. "That's the nicest thing you've ever said to me," she said.

Cal nodded and looked away.

I can't look at her without letting my thoughts be known, but I have to keep carrying on as I've been doing. I sure wish I didn't know how to read.

He knew she was anxious to hear from the judge but kept busy with teaching. Some nights he'd hold Charlie while she helped the children practice their handwriting and arithmetic. They liked working with numbers, and Jess made some simple cards for addition and subtraction. Then on to basic geography. Sarah watched and listened, and Cal wondered how much she was learning, too.

One day the snow began to melt, and the clear, blue sky overhead gave promise that spring was just around the corner. The townsfolk returned to building the church.

Cal offered to help a newcomer build a home in exchange for assistance when Cal was ready to start his house. He saw Jess driving by and marveled at how much she had changed since her arrival.

The last time they talked, she'd mentioned her fear of losing Charlie. "I'd think the judge would have answered my petition by now."

"They're busy. Not too many judges to serve eastern Oregon," Cal offered. "You'll hear. With the weather so bad this winter, it wouldn't have been a good idea to go all that way. I doubt the stagecoach would have come for you."

"I wonder when Lenny's coming back."

"I heard he's down in Harney County working for a sheep-herder," Cal said.

"I hope he stays there." Jess looked down at her knotted fists. "Oh, Abby." She shook her head. "There were so many things I should have said and didn't."

I think of things I could have said—should have said—to Millie, too. If I had it to do over, I'd tell her every day how much I loved her, how much she meant to me.

"Cal, I've been thinking about having a Sunday school class in the church while we're waiting for a preacher to come. Do you think that's a good idea?"

Cal nodded. "Yep, I do. The Downing children would come—"

"And fill up the class," Jess interrupted, "if Elias will let them."

"Doubt that any men would come though."

"Yes, I understand. They wouldn't take to a woman teaching anything."

"You can try." *I'll come. I don't care who's teaching.*

⁂

As Jess helped with supper preparations, she couldn't wait to see the building going up, couldn't wait to go inside and inspect the rough-hewn walls, stand where the preacher would stand, imagining rows of people listening, hearing the sounds of the piano being played. She stopped. But who would play the piano? She hadn't thought of that before. They must have a piano player. Perhaps she could advertise for one. The newspaper from Vale arrived on the incoming train. It carried classified ads for all sorts of things. Yes, she'd put an ad in for a pianist.

"You're so quiet today," Emma said, setting out a plate of

butter to go with her baking powder biscuits. "What's on your mind?"

Jess turned, her eyes shining. "I was thinking about the church and what a blessing it will bring to this valley."

"That it will, Jess—that it will."

Jess also looked forward to having her own home, knowing it was time to take full responsibility of Charlie. She brought him over to the boardinghouse mornings after class and some afternoons. Mrs. Downing had been most generous to feed him but couldn't be responsible for his life forever.

&

"Dudley Bowles is going back home—somewhere in Ohio, he said. He's had his fill of Western life and misses the opera," Cal mentioned over supper one evening.

"Misses the opera?" Jess's eyes twinkled with merriment. "That's what he said?"

"Yep. Sure did." Cal met her gaze, then felt that crazy thing happen to his heart again.

"I'm instrumental in seeing that a church is built here," Jess said, "but I don't think I could do anything about the opera."

"It will come one day perhaps."

"Or we may have to go to that town over in Idaho—what's it called?"

"Boise."

Cal had thought about taking over Dudley's house and acre of land. He wanted peace and quiet, which he did not get now. His first month in the Pell's Valley area, he'd boarded near the Stubblefield place, hiring out as a ranch hand. When no longer needed, he'd come to town and slept over the saloon. It would be wonderful to have his own house, but Jess needed it more.

"Is he moving all his stuff?" Emma asked.

"No. Leaving it. Said it'd take too much time to haul it back home. He'll sell the house and everything in it for three hundred."

He knew Jess had some money, but if she fixed the church

up the way she wanted to, she wouldn't have enough left.

"Been thinkin' of buying him out and using it or maybe renting it to someone." He looked at Jess and grinned.

"Cal"—Jess's smile widened—"I could be your first renter."

"Yep. Kinda had you in mind."

&

Jess was so excited she couldn't eat much of the noon meal. Her stomach was fluttering, and after pushing her food around on the plate, Emma took note.

"I sure hope you aren't coming down with that influenza I heard talk about. Seems a rash of it is going on west of here."

"I can't get sick now."

"You do look peaked though. Why don't you go take a nap?"

Jess climbed the stairs, ready for the comfort of her room. She would read a few verses, and perhaps that would lull her to sleep.

Prayers followed. Jess prayed for news about the hearing soon and that Cal would be able to buy the house. She thanked God for bringing her here, for meeting Cal, for the new church, and then for Charlie, sweet, wonderful Charlie. She had so many blessings, and sometimes she went through the day not taking time to be thankful.

"And, Lord, if it's Your will, I pray that I might find a new and fulfilled life as Cal Rutledge's wife. I haven't voiced it in so many words before, but that is the desire of my heart. I never realized it until this morning. Now if he can only think of me in that way and not love me because it's a way to see Charlie. I praise and thank You, dear God. Amen."

Gunshots and raised voices woke Jess an hour later. She sat up and pulled back the curtain to see what was going on.

Riding on horseback into the yard below were Lenny Thorne and three men, shouting and waving their rifles in the air.

"O Lord, help!" Jess breathed.

Then she heard a loud banging on the door and voices filling

the boardinghouse. "I want to see Miz Wilcox. Immediately."
She recognized Lenny's voice.

Jess sprang from bed, patted her hair into place, and slipped
into her boots.

"I'm coming!" she called out.

"I want my son, and I want him *now*." Lenny pointed a gun
at Jess as soon as she was downstairs.

"I don't have him."

He leered at her. "I know that. And that kid over there is
half-crazy. I'm not going there to get him. You have to do it."

"You can't just take him like that, Lenny. He's being fed and
cared for by Mrs. Downing. Please don't do this."

The men had been drinking, and Jess shrank back, remembering that one didn't argue with liquored-up men. She didn't
want Emma's kitchen smashed.

Lenny reached out, but Emma stepped between them. "I
won't have this in my house! You can settle this in a civilized
way, not like this."

"I'm not leaving until she comes with me."

"You're leaving, and you're leaving now," a gruff voice said.

Lenny whipped around and found a shotgun aimed at his
head. "What's going on here? And who are you?"

"Doesn't matter who I am. I work here, and I protect the
house and Miss Emma and anyone else who stays here."

Jess finally let herself breathe. It was Howard. He kept the
house running for Emma, fetched water, and ran errands,
whatever she needed. Jess had never felt so glad to see anyone
in her life.

Lenny backed up. "I don't usually argue with a shotgun—no
sirree."

"I suggest you leave then and take your friends with you."

Lenny didn't move. Howard took two steps forward. "I
mean *now*."

"You haven't heard the last of this, Jess." Lenny scowled at
her. "I aim to get my son, and I'll think of a way."

"Why not wait until the hearing in Vale?" Emma suggested. "Miss Wilcox is waiting for a date."

"Yeah, sounds likely. Waiting for how long?"

"Any day now," Jess said. "He'll hear both of our sides and come to a decision."

"Ha!" Lenny roared. "And how dumb do I look? What's a judge going to do—give custody to a cowboy like me or to a well-dressed, rich lady like you? C'mon—I'm not falling for that."

"It will be a fair trial," Jess said. "I believe that with all my heart."

"This isn't over," Lenny said, backing toward the door as Howard stepped toward him again.

After the door was closed and the sound of horses' hooves echoed in the distance, Jess crumpled. Emma rushed to her with smelling salts and helped her to the nearest chair. "Don't you worry none."

"Maybe I should just take Charlie and leave on the next train, as I was going to do in the first place."

"What? And not be here for the church dedication? Not see the church fill with people? Not be around to hear me play the piano?"

"*What* piano?" Jess's eyes widened. "*You* play the piano, Emma? I didn't know."

"I know you didn't, and I'm giving the piano in the parlor to the church. Nobody plays it much, and it's just collecting dust. Why not give it where it's needed?" She crossed her arms. "Besides, that's one expense you won't have."

"Oh, Emma." Jess reached up and hugged her elderly friend. "What would I do without you and—" She turned to look for Howard, but he'd already left.

"Howard's making sure they went in the right direction and not toward the Downings' cabin."

"Emma, I don't know what to say."

"Say? Say nothing. Just be glad you're here and not back

in Kansas baking bread for a certain man who doesn't appreciate you."

Jess smiled, her fingers touching the cross she wore around her neck. It was Abby's cross. The day Brady left Pell's Valley, she had taken the chain from the necklace he gave her and slipped her sister's cross on it. She felt better just by touching it, as if Abby were with her.

"That Mr. Thorne. He'll get into trouble at the saloon, and with some luck Sheriff Wall will have him in the hoosegow. You wait and see."

fifteen

The message came with the stagecoach driver on Monday.

"Custody hearing in the case of infant to be held in Malheur County Courtroom, Monday, March 19, at 2:00 p.m."

Jess stood on the sidewalk outside the general store and held the announcement in her hands. She had prayed for it to happen soon, and here it would be next week. Was she prepared? Hardly. Prayers had gone up all through Pell's Valley on her behalf, but somehow she didn't think she had a chance.

The afternoon sun warmed her face, and she lifted her heart to God for answered prayer. She glanced down at her faded muslin and smiled. She looked like a rancher's wife for sure. Her hair fell about her face in wisps; she had no time to fuss with it and had never felt better or more alive.

"There's something about helping others that is so rewarding," Jess said to Emma when the older woman stopped by to see how the church was coming along.

Emma nodded. "How true. Sometimes God puts us in the most unexpected places to be of use."

Jess pointed at the floor. "Livvy and I plan to varnish the floor tomorrow. And the material for the curtains is ordered."

"Never thought I'd see a church in these here parts. Just didn't seem possible. What a difference two people can make in a town."

"Two?" Jess looked puzzled.

"You and Cal."

"Oh."

Cal. Every time I hear his name, it's like warmth surrounds me. When he is around, everything goes right in my life.

122

"Cal arrived first."

"You both changed our town." Emma reached over and took Jess's hand. "See here. Calluses. I never thought I'd see the day when you looked like this, but it makes you fit right in."

"Now if we'd just hear from one of the preachers," Jess said, "that would help."

"It will come, dear. Give it time. And on that first Sunday when a preacher steps inside our little church, we need a dedication. And a party follows a dedication of the building. I'll donate the cake, coffee, and tea."

"Emma, you're such a blessing."

Her friend smiled as she headed for the door. "In the meantime, go ahead with your plans for the Sunday school. I've seen how changed the Downing children are, just from learning to read and write. You've instilled confidence in them by loving and accepting them."

"And Charlie. He recognizes everyone in town. He's so funny. His little legs kick, and he talks and smiles and—oh, Emma, what will I do if the judge gives him to Lenny?"

"Your heart will break, but we'll fight it."

"How can we do that?"

"You've heard of appeals?" Emma smiled. "Remember that my son practices law in Denver, Colorado, and will know what to do."

Jess nodded. "Yes, and 'don't borrow trouble,' as Mama used to say."

Emma left to do her shopping, and Jess watched her go. She loved the woman as a mother. She was wise and caring. Emma had come to Pell's Valley five years ago before either the store or the saloon was there. "I stayed because I felt needed," she'd explained when Jess asked one morning about the boardinghouse.

Stayed because I felt needed. Jess knew that was why she had stayed. That and Charlie and then Cal. And now the church.

A coat of varnish and the church would be finished. Jess

couldn't wait for her pupils to see the completed room. She wished they could have pews, but chairs would work for now.

A fire roared in the potbelly stove. Jess stood by it, taking in the warmth. Springtime was cold in Pell's Valley. She could hardly wait to see what summer was like, but she dreaded encountering the rattlesnakes she'd heard lived in the area.

"I'm here to help with the final varnishing." Livvy stood in the doorway, breaking through Jess's thoughts.

Jess turned and smiled. "You are such a dear to help. And your father doesn't mind your being away from the store?"

"Oh, no. I restocked shelves and did the books. The rest of the day is mine."

Jess started in one corner, Livvy in the opposite. They would work their way toward the door and end up there.

Livvy liked to chatter and figured Jess was a good listener, but on this day Jess's thoughts were again on Charlie. In less than a week she would know if Charlie was hers or if he'd be given to his father. She had prayed so long and hard that all she could do now was wait and see.

"The judge will see how honest and forthright you are, Miz Wilcox," Livvy said. "One look at that Lenny, and he'll know he's up to no good."

Jess smiled. "How did you know what I was thinking about?"

"I could tell. You sure weren't listening to me, and I know what is heavy on your heart."

"You are a perceptive young woman," Jess said. *And what might you tell me about Cal?* she wanted to ask. *I know you love him, Miss Olivia, but his heart isn't ready to give away. Not yet. Maybe never.*

"Lenny still claims he's a changed man." Jess stood, pressing on the kink in her lower back. "I want what's best for Charlie. If Lenny were stable and loving, I'd let him have the baby. According to my sister's letters, though, he is neither of those two."

They finished and stood looking at the shiny floor.

"I can help with the Sunday school class, if you want."

"I do, Livvy. You can pass out the Bibles."

"I'd better go now and see if Pa needs something."

Jess watched her walk across the street. Perhaps Livvy would make a better wife for Cal than she would. He hadn't shown the slightest bit of interest, however, and Jess saw nothing to make him change. He was busy with building his own house now. She didn't see him much, and it was strange how the feeling took over and stayed inside a person. She kept thinking the feeling would leave. Out of sight, out of mind, some might say; but it didn't happen that way. Try as she might, she couldn't fall out of love with Cal Rutledge.

Jess walked out and surveyed the building. She was still in awe over how fast it had gone up once the snow stopped. Pell's Valley Church. They'd have to make a sign. Funny that she hadn't thought of a sign until now.

She locked the door. She didn't trust Lenny. She walked toward home to the little house she'd cleaned and painted. Cal charged her a modest price for rent, and Emma insisted on paying most of it. "You've given me lessons and helped in the kitchen. You think I can't pay you a bit of a wage?"

The second oldest Downing girl, Dorothy, was taking care of Charlie, and she quickly gathered her things when she heard Jess come.

"Thank you," Jess said. "Did he wake up?"

"No, ma'am, he didn't."

Charlie had outgrown his cradle, so Cal had made a longer and wider bed of heavy oak. Four square legs made it higher so Jess didn't have to bend so low. She gazed at her sleeping nephew. His dark hair lay in ringlets across his forehead. She loved him so much, and the thought of having to give him up tore at her. What would she do without him? She had decided not to take him to Vale for the hearing. It would be a long trip. She'd leave at daybreak and stay overnight at the hotel. She wished Cal could come, too. She wanted support, someone there who understood, but he was building his house and expecting cattle to come in soon.

Charlie whimpered, and Jess smiled as she tickled him under the chin. She picked him up and held his face to her cheek. He pulled her hair and babbled in his baby talk way.

"You are getting so big. I can't believe it." Jess laid him down again and went to fix his food. "You're just a little pig." Her heart squeezed shut again as she wondered if Lenny would see that he was fed well. Who would care for him when Lenny worked?

Jess sat, holding Charlie until darkness crept around her little home. Curtains made from an old dress of Emma's hung at the windows. She rocked and hummed as she held Charlie tight. She never wanted the moment to go away. She'd cherish each hour she had Charlie, as it might be her last.

❧

Cal found another section of downed fence. "Probably caused by the last storm—it was a doozy," he said to Dover. The shack was cleaned out, and inside were enough supplies for him to get by on. With no bed there, he still used his bedroll. A table, the stove, and one chair furnished the room. Cobwebs still hung from corners, but things like that didn't bother him. Jess would have the place looking cleaner, he knew. Look at what she'd done for the church and her home. She had ordered drapes for the church windows. "To keep the cold out," she'd explained. Curtains were important to women.

Cal thought of how he got caught up in her excitement as she pointed out where the pulpit would go. "If everyone in town comes, we'll be crowded, but we can always build on later." Her blue eyes sparkled, and he fought the urge to pull her into his arms. "No telling what God will do in our little town," she went on.

No telling what God will do. The same could be said for Cal. He'd come thinking he'd never find anyone to marry, to have children with, and God had first dropped a baby in his lap and then brought a woman into his life. Not that anything was going to happen, for he could not speak his heart or tell of his intentions.

Besides, Jess continued to wear Brady's necklace around her neck, and as long as she did so, she must be thinking of him. She might still return to Kansas and Brady. The thought left him sad.

The wind whistled around the shack, and he blew out his kerosene lamp and prayed for God's will and guidance.

"Lord, I think it's a good thing You're in charge of my life. I would botch it up most likely. Is it too selfish to ask for the desires of my heart? Is it right that I should want Jess for my wife? And Charlie for my son?"

After praying, Cal tried to listen, not that he'd ever heard an audible voice, but he often felt the nudge to do something. This time it came through clearly. It was as if God were saying, "You have unfinished business, My son. It's time to seek forgiveness from your brother. Go to him. Ask for it."

Cal bolted up. *Go see Tom? I should go and tell him I'm sorry? But I did that, and all I got was a slamming door and my brother's refusal to accept my apology as he stalked off.*

They should have shaken hands, hugged, or made amends in some way. But they hadn't.

Now as Cal sat there, staring into the dark night, he knew that before he could get on with his life, he had to try to make peace one more time. And he'd been thinking of Millie a lot lately. He loved her still, yet the strong sense of that love was fading with each passing day. Was it time to let her go, too? When he went to Montana to see his brother, he'd go to her grave site and have a talk. He had to do this. He knew it was what God was asking of him. Then and only then would he be ready to think about Jess, to fight Brady for her hand.

Dover whinnied loudly, a whinny of distress from the far end of the shack. Cal grabbed his boots and rifle and went outside. A fine film of snow covered the fire he'd built last night, but the eyes of an animal several yards from the campsite caught his attention.

He aimed his rifle and shot as the animal turned to run. He got him in the back and, not wanting it to suffer, fired again. The wolf fell.

Shivering, Cal patted Dover and gave him a handful of oats. "Good boy."

He went back inside the lean-to; but it took a long time to get warm again, and he tossed and turned for several minutes before sleep came.

sixteen

"Bring them in. Bring them in—bring the wandering ones to Jesus!" Jess sang, watching Emma's fingers fly over the keys.

The church had a piano and a pianist, a shiny floor, hymnals and Bibles, and people with smiles on their faces, singing with gusto. All they needed was a preacher, but one would be coming. Jess knew it in her heart.

Tomorrow she would know the judge's decision concerning Charlie. If only Cal could go with her. But for now she would try to put the next morning out of her mind.

When Cal entered five minutes later, Henry Downing stood and motioned for him to take his seat, the only one remaining. Cal took it and nodded to Henry.

"I'm going to tell you the story of David, a little shepherd boy," Jess said.

She carefully avoided Cal's gaze, instead concentrating on Livvy, who held Charlie. The baby was passed around during the Sunday school program, and soon Cal had him. Charlie now focused on faces, and when he recognized someone, he gurgled.

Jess felt the old tugging at her heart as she watched Cal with the baby. Lenny could never give that kind of love. He might be a father, but it didn't make him a loving one.

Livvy stood and read the Twenty-third Psalm, then sat down.

Emma started pounding out the closing hymn, "We Gather Together."

After the service, Emma invited Cal, Jess, and Livvy to the boardinghouse for the noon meal. "I put the ham on early this morning. There's enough for all."

"Where was your father this morning?" Jess asked Livvy.

"He has to mind the store."

"Maybe he could close it for an hour. Everyone—almost everyone—was at the Sunday school service."

"He says he's getting used to the idea. He'll close it when the preacher comes."

Emma laughed. "And he who waits sometimes waits too long. Waiting until judgment day is not a good idea."

The afternoon sun blazed out of a cobalt blue sky as the party of four made their way to the boardinghouse. Another house was going up beyond Emma's and several on the other side of the Downings'. Progress was coming to Pell's Valley. Soon the church would be too full, and they'd need to add on a room. That would please Jess immensely.

Cal asked the blessing for the food, and Jess caught Livvy looking at him admiringly. Would Cal wake up one day and realize Livvy loved him? And if he did, what would he do? He needed a mate; he was such a loving and giving man.

"Are you ready for the hearing?" Cal asked her when they were drinking coffee and enjoying slices of Emma's cherry pie.

"Yes, I'm leaving in the morning, you know."

"The stage arrives at five o'clock," Emma said. "I'll be up to cook Jess a good breakfast."

Jess felt fear closing in and tried to push it aside. If only it could be over with, she would feel much better.

"Maybe Mr. Thorne won't be there," Livvy said. "I've heard of that happening."

"Oh, he'll be there," Emma said. "He wouldn't miss out on that, not when he wants his son."

Jess thought of Abby's letter again. The words still chilled her to the bone. *I need to get out of here. Lenny is selling everything he can get his hands on. I'll probably be next.*

"Yes, I think he'll be there," Cal agreed. "My prayers go with you."

Charlie stretched from the pallet on the floor, breaking the tense mood. Jess went to him, burying her face in his blanket. She had to hold him every chance she had, cling to him, watch the way his eyes opened and he smiled when he recognized her. *How could I ever give him up?*

"I must get back to help Pa," Livvy said. "We have in some pretty fabrics. Stop by one day, Jess."

Cal walked Livvy to the door, and Jess watched him. She so wanted to talk to him, wanted him to know how scared she was. What if she ran off with the baby tonight? She would go in the opposite direction; but she'd need a horse, and the thought of carrying a baby made her realize she couldn't handle it. Besides, it was running from her problem, and she would not do that. She must trust God in this. And He had impressed on her to forgive Lenny. What if God told her to give up the baby? It'd be like the woman in the book of Kings. She'd wait for the judge's decision. All she could do was pray and wait.

Cal came back in and nodded toward Emma. "Sure was good cherry pie," he said.

"Have another piece," Emma said. "I know you're clamoring for it. And remind me to order an extra box of canned cherries for the next shipment on the train."

She poured more coffee and set the last slab of pie in front of Cal. But he didn't pick up his fork. He watched Jess. "You're certainly quiet."

Jess nodded, holding the baby closer. "I know." She didn't look up. "My mother always said if you have problems bigger than you can manage, consider your brother, because his problem might be heavier than yours."

"So is that what you're doing?" Cal asked.

"Yes."

Emma finished clearing the table and came to sit. "Whose problems are you thinking of?"

Jess's face reddened as she held on to Charlie's finger. He had such a grip for one so young. He gurgled at her, and she tickled his fat little tummy.

"Some people love and lose their loved one. Some never find anyone to love at all. And some are not blessed with the gift of children."

"Well, that covers quite a lot of us," Emma said.

Cal pushed his empty plate aside. "I belong in two of those categories."

"And I belong to all three," Jess said.

"You're young," Emma scoffed. "You'll find love one day—"

"Will I, Emma? How will I know?"

"One knows, believe me. One knows."

Cal's chair scraped back. "I have one last fence to build."

"I was surprised you came in today," Jess said.

"How could I miss Sunday school?" His gaze captured and held hers.

Jess smiled. "It was nice of you to come."

"Nice of you to help me eat the ham and clean up the cherry pie," Emma added.

Jess suddenly placed Charlie in Cal's arms. "Here—it may be the last time you get to hold him."

"Yep, I love this little guy," he said.

"I know you do."

Moments after the door closed, Jess took Charlie and fled up the stairs to her room. If she hurried, she could watch Cal leaving from the window, and somehow she needed that visualization right now.

❧

Cal wanted to go to Vale for the hearing. He'd thought about it more than once. He could rise before dawn and ride over first thing in the morning. Would his presence help? If the judge asked for witnesses, he could voice his thoughts on the matter.

It was midafternoon when he headed out across the flat land toward his ranch. He thought of what was really at stake here. A child needed a good home. Jess could provide that much better than the ne'er-do-well Lenny Thorne. Lenny couldn't care for himself, much less a baby. He'd had a wife and left her alone. She'd had to work to have food and a place to stay. Would the judge know all that? Would Lenny have someone to present his case? Cal should have suggested that Jess have legal representation, but Pell's Valley had none.

A heavy south wind blew up by the time Cal reached his makeshift home. He started a fire and felt the chilly night air coming on. Somehow he doubted he'd sleep much tonight. Thoughts of Jess kept racing through his mind. She needed someone there on her side. Cal needed her in his life, but how could he bring it up when she was worried and upset about Charlie? *First things first, I know.*

Cal had drawn plans for the house. They were crude plans, but they served his purposes. Over the fading light of day, he looked at the drawing.

Living room, large kitchen, two bedrooms, and a lean-to for storage. He'd order windows from Boise and a special front door. He wanted oak, but pine cost less. He also wanted a pitched roof, though he didn't need to worry about a roof caving in. The constant wind caused snow to pile up along fences and in drifts along the road. One day he would paint the wood, not leave it to gray and weather. White was his choice. At the thought of white, he remembered Millie's dream—that of building a house and having a white picket fence. She also wanted yellow roses in the front yard. She hadn't lived long enough to realize the dream, and for that Cal was sorry. If he were ever to marry again, he'd do his best to see that his wife's dreams were fulfilled.

What would happen if Jess lost Charlie? Would she leave on the first train? Nothing was keeping her here. He wished something was, but now that the church was built and she'd gotten things started, she would undoubtedly return to Kansas. If only she wouldn't keep wearing that necklace. As long as she did, he knew he didn't have a chance.

Then there was Livvy. Cal liked the young girl, but not

in the way she wanted. She was only eighteen, eleven years younger than him, and needed a fellow closer to her age. He hoped she would find someone.

When Jess flashed through his mind again, Cal knew he had to go to Vale. He had one clean shirt and a clean pair of dungarees, and tonight he'd spit-polish his boots. He didn't want to drive Dover too hard, but getting up early would give him plenty of time to make the two o'clock hearing. That meant riding back after dark, but he'd do it. He used to ride in the dark all the time in Montana. He'd have his saddlebags full of food and his rifle for protection.

"Lord," he prayed quietly, "let me help if I can tomorrow. Then let me go and find forgiveness from Tom. Help me show peace and love. And please let Jess get custody of Charlie; then maybe one day she will look at me and know I am the husband for her."

Coyotes called back and forth as they paced a mile or so from the campfire, but Cal drifted off anyway.

seventeen

"But the salvation of the righteous is of the Lord: He is their strength in the time of trouble."

Jess had marked the psalm the night before and gone to sleep with those words on her mind and in her heart. Now as she dressed in the darkness, she prayed for the Lord's will and was grateful the hearing would be over soon.

She had wanted Cal to stay yesterday. Whenever she was with him, she wanted time to stand still.

After breakfast Emma shoved a cup of hot tea in her hand, then put a sack lunch on the table beside her. Charlie, still asleep in his new bed, didn't stir as Jess wrapped up in her heaviest cloak and donned the gray bonnet with the wide brim. She wanted to look her best.

The sound of the stagecoach filled the quiet morning air, a morning too dark for even the birds to sing. The driver helped her into the coach.

"Are you comfortable, ma'am?"

"Yes, thank you."

Jess tried to keep her teeth from chattering. Whoever had said it was the coldest at dawn knew what they were talking about. Even her woolen gloves didn't help. Her fingers already felt like frozen stubs.

The driver locked the door and hopped up on the platform, and soon they had traveled some distance from Pell's Valley.

Jess felt herself drifting off to sleep. Then the coach would lurch and the driver would jerk on the reins, and she'd waken to find they barely missed a hole in the rough, rocky road.

Daylight filtered through the windows, now dirty from dust. Oh, how she wanted the trip to end. Jess's stomach rumbled from hunger, and she remembered the food Emma had packed. Perhaps she could share it with the driver: chunks of thick bread spread with lots of butter and homemade cherry preserves, sliced ham from the day before, and three cookies. Emma always had cookies on hand. These were oatmeal, Jess's favorite.

She ate one piece of bread and half the ham.

They crossed over a creek. On the other side the driver stopped the stagecoach and climbed down, then opened the door.

"Ma'am, you doing all right?"

Jess assured him she was and held out the bag. "Would you like to share my breakfast?"

"No, thank you, ma'am. I brought my own."

The sun was high in the sky when they reached the outskirts of Vale. Jess looked at her watch. It was twelve thirty. She would have enough time to stretch and freshen up a bit before the hearing. It was good they'd left as early as they had.

Vale was large compared to Pell's Valley. The courthouse dominated one block, and Jess shivered as they passed it. The fate of her life, of her sister's child, lay in the hands of the judge inside that building. Oh, she prayed for that decision.

"Ma'am, here we are," the driver said, helping her out of the coach. "This is the hotel. You have time to rest, if you want."

The town made her think more of her home in Kansas. People strolled along the boardwalks—women in hats and fine gowns of bombazine, not muslin like back in Pell's Valley.

"I'll be ready first thing in the morning for the trip back." He tipped his hat.

"And thank you for getting me here safely."

Jess held her skirt high to avoid a muddy spot along the edge of the walk. She hurried into the hotel and found her room, then straightened her dress and washed her face and hands in the basin provided. She wouldn't rest though, because she could only think of going into the courthouse. She would find where the hearing was to be held, then wait for the hour to come.

The granite walls and floor were beautiful but cold. How she wished everything were over. How she wished she were home in Kansas. She stopped.

Home in Kansas? Do I really want that? No. My home is in Pell's Valley, and even if I can't keep Charlie, my home and heart are there.

She sat on one of the smooth wooden benches and tried to keep her hands from trembling. The gloves, her warmest, were not her finest, and she hoped the judge would not notice. Jess leaned back and closed her eyes. Was Lenny already here? Would the door open and he suddenly appear? What would she say if he did? She crossed her ankles, wishing she could talk to someone. It helped to talk to Emma. Cal also lent comfort in situations, but she had no one here. For one of the few times in her life, she felt desolate and alone.

The words *"Lo, I am with you"* went through her mind.

"Yes, Lord, You are with me. I have to draw on Your strength now, because I could not do this by myself."

A door opened, and a young woman with pink cheeks and a plaid dress stepped into the hall. "May I help you?"

Jess nodded. "I'm waiting for a hearing about my nephew. Do you know where that might be?"

"Come with me. You're early, but I can show you the room."

Jess willed her legs to hold her up as she walked down the hall.

The woman opened a door. "This is for hearings. If this were a trial, you'd be in the next room."

"May I go in now?" Jess asked.

"Of course. The judge will expect you to be up front, so that's where you'll want to sit."

Jess thanked her and went in and sat down. The room was smaller than she'd anticipated. The Oregon flag and the American flag were hanging from one corner. The judge's bench was on a platform, a yard or so higher. Jess sighed and leaned back.

She wondered how Charlie was faring, wondered if he missed her. She knew Emma would take good care of him and Dorothy would help when Emma fixed a meal for the only other boarder.

So far she saw no sign of Lenny. Maybe he'd had a late start. Maybe he wouldn't show. If that happened, she'd win by default. Wasn't that what Livvy had said earlier?

Somehow Jess got through the next hour. Occasionally the door opened, and someone called out, "Are you waiting for Judge Lewis?"

"Yes, I am."

"It's going to be awhile. He's often late in getting back from lunch."

The next time the door opened, Jess knew it was Lenny. She knew without looking. She'd heard two sets of footsteps stomping down the hall, and then voices filled the room. Jess heard the grating tone in his words and trembled.

"Well, look at who's here. If it isn't Miz Wilcox herself."

Jess turned toward the front of the room as Lenny sidled up to her, his friend behind him. She smelled liquor on his breath and recoiled. She'd smelled that the first time they'd met back in Kansas. She'd known then he was up to no good. Why had he involved Abby?

He walked in front of her now, swaggering. She swallowed. He looked nice. For Lenny that must have been hard. A dark suit concealed his broad shoulders, and he wore a white shirt. It was soiled on one side, but the judge might not notice that. His cowboy hat was off, and his dark hair was slicked back with some sort of cream.

"You're looking good as always," he said, half-leering at her.

Jess glanced away. She wanted to ask who his friend was, certain it couldn't be his lawyer, as he would have introduced himself.

Tell him you forgive him, an inner voice said to her.

I can't, Jess thought. *I can't forgive him.*

But you must.

Jess turned to look at Lenny. Beneath his boastful air he appeared frightened. "Lenny, I'm sorry for my feelings toward you. After Abby died I blamed you, and it was wrong. Please forgive me."

He sputtered for a moment, then managed to say, "I'm sorry she had to die that way. Truly I am."

Jess bit back the tears that threatened. She felt as if a weight had been lifted from her. She also knew that no matter what happened, she had done the right thing.

At five minutes after two o'clock, a door in the front of the room opened and a young man came out with a Bible. He set it on the table. Another door opened, and a man garbed in a black robe entered.

"All rise," the first man said.

Jess held her head high as she rose to her feet. She grabbed the back of the bench in front of her for support. She'd never felt so scared in her life.

The judge nodded and motioned for everyone to sit down. He scanned the papers in front of him and glanced up at Jess and Lenny, then back down at the papers.

"Jess," a voice behind her said softly.

She turned quickly to see Cal standing there. *Cal came? He's here?*

"Sorry I'm late," he whispered. "I'll sit behind you."

It doesn't matter. Nothing matters except that you are here. I needed you far more than I realized.

"In the custody hearing of Miss Jessida Wilcox and Mr. Leonard Thorne, I must ask a few questions," the judge said.

Cal touched Jess's shoulder and whispered again before he sat down. "It's going to be fine."

"I'd like for each of you to tell your story and why you think you should have custody of this child—let's see—Charles Adam Thorne, age four months." He looked at Jess and motioned. "You may speak first, Miss Wilcox."

Jess felt terror filling her, but she had to speak in an audible voice and say the right thing.

O dear God, help me. Her hands still gripped her sides as she looked at the judge. One had to look a judge in the eye. Emma had told her that.

"I am Charlie's aunt. My sister, Abigail, is—*was*—his mother. She died giving birth to Charlie. He was found in an abandoned shack and brought to town, where Mrs. Sarah Downing began to nurse him—"

The judge waved his hand. "We can dispense with the details," he said. "I need to know why *you* want the child."

Why I want the child? Jess cried inwardly. *That should be obvious.* She finally found her voice. "I want him because my sister said I should have all of her possessions, and this child was hers—"

"A person isn't considered a possession," the judge cut in.

Jess felt her hopes die.

"Go on—tell him why you want Charlie," Cal encouraged her quietly.

"I love Charlie, and I think he needs a mother more than a father—at least a father who won't be there and can't provide for him."

"Now wait a minute!" Lenny barked. "That ain't true—"

"Hold on, young man. Your turn is next. Please—no more outbursts or I may have you removed from the court."

Lenny sat down, and Jess went on.

"I've taken care of Charlie since arriving in Pell's Valley, and I have a home. Charlie has his own bed, and he knows me better than anyone else."

Except for maybe Cal, she wanted to say.

"Are there grandparents in the picture?"

"No, sir. I am the only living relative."

"And you are not married?"

"That's correct."

"Don't you think a child needs both a mother and a father?"

"Yes, under ideal circumstances, but a mother gives more when the child is young, Your Honor."

"So when the child reaches ten or so, you think he could go live with his father?"

"Now just a minute!" Lenny exclaimed, jumping to his feet again. "He's my son, and I want him now."

"Mr. Thorne, I warned you."

"Sorry." Lenny slumped into his chair again.

"Now, as I was saying, would you be willing to let the child go to the father on visitation?"

Jess felt tears form in her eyes. How could she agree to that? She knew Lenny would take him far away and she'd never see him again.

"I don't know how it would benefit the child."

"I see."

The judge turned to Lenny. "It's your turn now, Mr. Thorne."

Lenny stood, his back straight. "It's my kid, Judge, and a child belongs with his father, not an aunt. Abby died unexpectedly, and I'm sorry I wasn't there for her, but I've changed. I've got a home, too, and a good job on a ranch. And there's someone to watch 'Charlie,' as she calls him."

"And would you be willing to let Miss Wilcox have visiting rights?"

Lenny hesitated for a long moment. "I suppose I could do that."

"I'll go over this in my chambers and return with my verdict shortly."

Jess breathed a deep sigh. The difficult part was over. She'd done her best, but Lenny had sounded convincing, too. How could the judge decide?

Cal slipped up and sat beside her. "You sounded good."

"I was scared."

"Yep, could tell by the tremor in your voice."

"Oh, Cal, what do you think will happen?"

"Hard to say."

She turned and met his gaze. "Thank you for coming."

Ten minutes later the judge came out of his chambers. At the same moment the courtroom door burst open, and two men in uniform, a sheriff and a deputy, rushed in.

"And what is the reason for this intrusion?" the judge said, standing there, papers in hand.

"We're looking for someone and were told he might be here."

"Who is this someone?"

"His name is Leonard Thorne. Seems he was working down in Harney County, helping out a sheepherder, and took all his life's savings."

"You must have proof—"

Lenny tried to slip out the side door, but the sheriff stopped him before he could escape. "Yes, I'm sure you're the man we want." He pinned Lenny's arms behind him. "What's this bulge here?"

The sheriff pulled a wad of bills from Lenny's coat pocket, and the judge banged his gavel.

"I don't think I need more time to deliberate. I find the child, Charles Adam, will go to the aunt, Miss Jessida Wilcox."

As the door closed behind Lenny, Jess sank to the bench and let the tears fall. God had answered her prayers in more ways than one. Lenny was shown for who and what he was, and Cal had come to be with her at this awful time. She turned and smiled through her tears.

"He's mine," she whispered, touching Cal's hand. "All mine, thank the Lord."

❧

Jess arrived back in Pell's Valley the next day at noon.

Cal had arrived earlier and waited at Emma's.

Jess couldn't wait to grab Charlie and squeeze him tight. "We're okay, Charlie. I'm so sorry, baby, but your daddy is in jail. At least for now." She turned and took Cal's hand. "If it weren't for you, I wouldn't be here, nor would Charlie be alive. I would have had to visit two grave sites. I can't thank you enough."

"This calls for a celebration," Emma said. "And I've baked the very cake to serve!"

eighteen

Once Cal's mind was made up about returning to Montana, he felt a deep sense of peace. Maybe Tom wouldn't forgive him. Even if he didn't, it would still be worth the trip. Cal wanted to see the ranch, find out if his old dog, Brownie, was still alive, and visit and talk over things with Millie at the grave site. He also wanted to see George, a friend in town who worked with wood and constructed beautiful works of art.

As the train headed east and then north, a thought was growing in the back of Cal's mind: pews for the church. George's craftsmanship would be remarkable, and Jess would be so pleased. He could see her clasping her hands in pleasure now. Bittersweet memories came flooding back as the train pulled into the Moosehead station.

On seeing his old friend, he learned George's hands were too arthritic to work anymore. He held up his knobby knuckles and shook his head.

"It pains me, boy, not to work with these hands. But God was good to me for many years. I have to content myself with sitting back and enjoying my twilight years."

Cal felt disappointed but thanked George anyway. He was heading out the door when the old man called to him.

"Just remembered something, son."

"Yes?" Cal turned and waited.

"I have some wood I ordered before my hands got so bad. It's out in the shed. Let's go take a look and see if it would be good for what you want. Pews, you say?"

"Yes."

The wood was a heavy oak, and George insisted that Cal take it. "I'd feel honored to think my wood made pews for a tiny church in a cow town in Oregon."

Cal made arrangements to pick it up for the train ride home. Already his mind was whirling with possibilities. Young Henry liked to whittle. He was also good with his hands. Just maybe. . .

As Cal walked through town to the livery, his heart started to beat faster. A woman in a dark dress sauntered down the walk, reminding him of Millie. They'd had such a short time together. Sometimes it seemed the memory was fading, while other times it was as if they'd met only yesterday.

Things had changed. A new building graced Main Street, and several horses stood at the hitching post. Cal rented a pinto to ride out to the ranch. He hadn't told Tom he was coming. He thought it would be better to surprise him.

The rolling meadows made his heart constrict. He'd forgotten how beautiful it was with the snowcapped mountains looming in the west. That was why his father had picked this place for his ranch. Millie had loved the scenery and spent those early months of carrying their child strolling over the land, gathering bouquets of the tiny daisies. By the end of summer, the green meadows would be brown.

Cal stopped, gathered up as many daisies as his hand could hold, and swung back on his horse. He was ready to go to the grave now.

He took the ride slowly, breathing in the smells of Montana. It was different from Oregon's high desert, but as the painful memories continued, Cal was sure he had made the right decision.

Should he go to the house first or to Millie's grave site? Since it was closer and the sun had already begun its western descent, he plodded up the hill and toward the grove of yellow pines. He had chosen the most beautiful spot on the ranch. If he could have, he'd have buried Millie in the middle of the meadow, but that wouldn't be practical. He knew she liked the pines as well. Millie was like that, easy to please.

The small family plot was enclosed with a split rail fence. Cal slipped off his horse and tied the reins around a post. He'd need to get oats for the horse before riding back to the farmhouse. He had hoped he would be welcome for a night or two before returning to Pell's Valley.

He'd forgotten the scent of new green grass this time of year and breathed deeply. He gazed up at the wide expanse of blue sky with a thin layer of puffy clouds. He had to admit he missed the big sky of Montana.

Cal opened the gate and went in. Millie's grave was on the far side, and he found it with no problem. He bent down to read the small stone, the size he could afford at the time. He'd carved Millie's name in the stone—he hadn't put Mildred, her real name, since she disliked it. She said she was named for her mother, but she hadn't known her parents. They'd died in a flu outbreak back east when she was two. A neighbor had taken in Millie, and when she grew up, she went west to find adventure. She stopped at Moosehead and found a job at the local café. Cal lumbered in one morning, and it was love at first sight.

"Millie, I need to talk." Cal placed the daisies at the foot of the stone. "And you know I never was much for talking. I miss you more than I could ever imagine, yet I know you and our son are in a better place." The two-day-old baby had lain in Millie's arms in the casket, but Cal hadn't put his name on the stone. He hadn't known what to call him. Before his birth he and Millie had clashed on a name. Cal wanted to name him Blaine after his father, but Millie wanted him to be Calvin Jr.

Cal removed his hat and placed it over his chest. "Millie, I have a new life, a new home now, and I've met someone—her name is Jess—actually Jessida. I don't know if she'll even have me, but I aim to find out when I return. I just want you to know you'll always hold my heart in your hands, and I'll keep part of you deep inside, as that is how it should be with first loves. I loved you so much. If we'd taken you to the hospital in

Helena, you might have lived. I'll always have regrets for that.

"But you're not alone. Our baby comforts you as you comfort him. And I'm going to call him Calvin Jr. as you wanted. It seems right for that to be his name now."

Cal bent down on one knee and closed his eyes. "Thank You, God, for Millie and for my time with her. And now, Lord, please let me know You send Your blessing and what You want me to do. I've strayed from You in the past but have always claimed you as my God. Amen."

Cal's stubby fingers traced the name, and he leaned over and kissed the granite. "Take care, Millie, and good-bye."

Going to his horse, Cal didn't look back. It was time to look forward. He must continue with his new life.

He headed down the hill, through the grove of aspen, then heard the familiar bark. Brownie, getting on in years, still ran like lightning.

"Brownie, ol' boy!" Cal clamored down from his horse, and the dog bounded onto him, licking his face, his ears, sniffing and nosing his pocket the way he used to, looking for a treat.

"I didn't bring a treat," Cal said, scratching the dog's ears. "Guess I forgot all about it. But you sure didn't."

Then he saw Tom riding up the hill. The sudden coolness in the air told him night would come soon. That meant supper, and Tom could cook some mighty tasty food.

"Cal, is it really you?"

Tom pounded him on the back as they stepped back and stared at each other.

"I thought it had to be you. Nobody else ever goes over that way. The cattle are east of here. And then when I saw Brownie take off—" Tom hesitated. "Man, you're looking good."

"And you, little brother, have grown even taller."

Tom shrugged. "Some of us keep growing until we die. I may be eight foot before they bury me."

"Tom, we need to talk."

Tom's face darkened. "Well, sure. You didn't come just to see

Millie, now did you?"

Cal felt a sudden chill, and his resolve faltered.

"S'pose you're movin' back—"

"No." Cal met his brother's gaze. "Of course you'd think that. Why else would I come all this way? But no, I've bought a ranch in Oregon."

"You have?"

"Yep."

"You like it there?"

"Yep, sure do."

Tom leaned down to ruffle Brownie's ears. "I've worked hard here, making the ranch pay."

"I'm sure you have, Tom."

Tom motioned toward the farmhouse. "Let's go inside. We can talk more, and I'll make some supper."

After full plates of beef and potatoes, Tom poured coffee and cut big slabs of buttermilk pie.

"You sure you ain't coming back?"

Cal glanced around the familiar kitchen and could visualize his mother cooking breakfast. "This will always be home; but it's yours, and I sure haven't come back to claim anything."

"Wouldn't blame you if you did. We parted on bad terms—"

"Yep, we did." Cal finished his coffee and pushed the cup aside. "And that's why I'm here."

"Figured as much."

"I heard a person speak once about forgiveness—"

"Say no more." Tom reached over and gripped Cal's shoulder. "No words are necessary." He nodded. "We have a lot of catching up to do. How long can you stay, brother?"

Brother. If only Tom knew how good that sounds.

"A night or two. I want to make it back for the Friday train into Pell's Valley. Expecting a shipment of furniture."

"Wish you could stay longer," Tom said. "Then you could meet my wife."

"Your *wife?*"

"Yeah. We're building us another house—this will be for the hired hands."

Cal stood and pounded his brother on the back. "That's great news! Do I know her?"

"Nah. She moved here right after you left. I was depressed, lonely, wondering if I even wanted the farm anymore, when Laura came into my life."

"Laura. Nice name."

"She loves the ranch. Loves to ride the range with me. She even helps round up the calves if a mother dies. Can you imagine this—last month after a huge snowstorm, she found a little heifer almost dead. She brought it home, put it in the tub, and got in with it to warm it. Now where could you find someone like that?"

"I'm happy for you, Tom. All I wanted was for you to find happiness like I had with Millie. I'm sorry for being such a jerk."

"Forget it. I'm sorry for not accepting your apology before you left. That's where Laura is good for me. She's made me talk about things I had buried inside me—and I know she'll want to meet you. She's in Idaho—her father's real sick. Probably dying."

"Sorry to hear that, but I need to get back to meet the train. Got a boy watching over the place. He's young but good. It's his mother who kept Charlie alive."

"Charlie?"

"Yep. I found a baby just been born, mother dying, out in the middle of nowhere on my south section. Brought the little feller into town, and he's thriving. His aunt—name is Jess—came from Kansas and claimed him, and she's still there."

"And this Jess—you love her, brother. I can tell."

Cal felt his heart quicken. "Yeah, that I do. Had to come talk to Millie about it. She's been so much a part of me, even after she died. And God is back in my life. How about you, Tom?"

Tom's face brightened. "I accepted the Lord as my Savior right after I met Laura. Never been happier or more content."

"God has a way of righting our lives, making good things happen."

"Are you going to marry this Jess?"

"She was engaged to a fellow back in Kansas. He came out at Christmas."

"And?"

"And then he went home."

"But she stayed."

"Yep, she stayed."

"You don't know why?"

"It's because of Charlie—the baby."

Tom lit the hurricane lamps and blew out the match. "That's the only reason?"

"Don't know for sure."

"Then you need to return and find out."

Later, after Cal went to his old room where he'd slept as a kid, his thoughts returned to his childhood, an earlier time of happiness. Cal was the oldest boy, and when he was nine, Tom was born. He remembered resenting the newborn brother, but his mother seemed to understand and sent him to live with his grandparents that summer. He missed the farm and his mother so much, but especially his father, that he went back and was never resentful again. Then he felt the responsibility of being the older brother and taught Tom about cattle and how to whittle and play a Jew's harp and answered dozens of questions. The older Tom got, the more questions he had.

Cal felt a closeness to Millie there, remembering her softness, her gentle ways. But he had to let her go. Life was for the living.

Morning came early, and Tom was out rousting up breakfast when Cal entered the kitchen.

"Thought you might like to look the place over after we eat. Let's take Maribel instead of the nag you rented."

Cal laughed. "Good ol' Maribel. Is she still the spitfire she once was? I hope not."

"Nah. She's a good ol' gal now—simmered down some. But you can get her riled up if you want."

"I think not."

They left with canteens after breakfast. Tom's spread was larger than Cal's in Oregon. Riding side by side, Cal saw the new fence at the north end and the beginning of Tom and Laura's house. It was built from rough-hewn logs, and Cal thought of his house. It would be nothing compared to Tom's, but that was all right.

"You've got a nice house going here. Wish I could be here for the housewarming."

"Yeah, I wish that, too."

"I'm happy for you, Tom. I really am. Just wish Dad were here to see the changes and how hard you've worked to make this a real ranch."

"I like to think he knows."

"Just as I felt Millie's presence those first terrible months after her death."

"Yeah, that was bad. I should have understood better. You weren't yourself. You lost not only your wife, but your baby son as well. I'm sorry for that loss."

"Thank you, little brother." He took in a deep breath of pine. "I'm ready to return to Pell's Valley, to finish building my house, propose to Jess, and get on with my life."

"Better to find out where you stand than to wonder about it, Cal."

They parted friends. Brothers. And believers.

Cal felt lighthearted as he made his way back to Moosehead to catch the train that would carry him to Pell's Valley. Chances were he and his brother would never see each other again. It was too far to travel, and he'd be busy with his ranch once he got his cattle. He was content in Oregon, as all thoughts of returning to Montana left his mind. He had made his life in Pell's Valley, and that's where he'd stay.

nineteen

Jess missed Cal while he was gone, but she included him in her prayers each morning. "Please, Lord, if it is Your will, let this be a good trip for Cal. He needs to mend fences with his brother. Needs to visit his wife's grave site. Then maybe things will come together."

The morning after Cal left, Jess reviewed the Sunday school material that had come in on the train. Her former church had sent last year's lessons, but that didn't matter to children who had never heard God's Word at all.

Jess had added one more person to her reading class: Howard, Emma's most trusted employee. He caught on quickly, too.

Jess walked to the church building that morning and sat in one of the front chairs. Soon they would need more. They'd already used all the chairs Jack Preston had in the store. She still had money left. If she didn't order the new bed she was thinking about, she'd have enough for two pews. She walked out into the sunny morning as the train whistle sounded. Jess shivered in anticipation. *Cal is coming home. Cal is coming home.*

Livvy and Jack soon joined Jess on the platform, and Dorothy came carrying Charlie. She handed him to Jess. "He's been a-fussing all morning. Why do you suppose that is?"

Jess laughed and held the chubby baby close. "Babies get like that sometimes." She reached over and hugged the younger girl. "You're a great helper, and I appreciate you so much."

Dorothy beamed and took Jess's hand. "Thank you," she murmured.

"You're welcome," Jess answered. Jess had enjoyed throwing in manners with one of her lessons, and so far Dorothy was her best pupil.

⠦

Cal looked out the train window as it chugged into the station. He saw Jess first, and his heart leapt. She waved, and he waved back. She was more beautiful than he remembered, and it had only been a week since he'd seen her. He had one thing in particular on his mind and prayed for the courage to say what he must.

He was also excited about the oak George had given him for the pews. He had plans for one piece—a sign for the church—so Jess would have two surprises. He pictured it now: Pell's Valley Community Church.

Then next week the first shipment of cattle was coming. He'd bring Henry in to help with that.

Cal was the only passenger to leave the train, and he sprang down the steps and crossed the platform to the little group. He reached for Charlie and hugged him hard. "Sure missed y'all," he said, looking over the baby's head, catching Jess's expression. *What does that look mean?* Charlie chortled, grabbing Cal's nose.

"He's getting to be a handful," Cal said. He saw the necklace gleaming in the sunshine, and his heart sank. *Brady's necklace. She's still wearing it.*

⠦

Jess had gone over in her mind a hundred times what she would say when Cal returned. She would tell him the truth. She loved him. And she'd finally realized he was the main reason for her staying in Pell's Valley. Wasn't it better to say what one felt than to skirt an issue?

But he had reached for Charlie. As she'd known all along, he cared only for Charlie. It wouldn't have mattered who stood there, as long as that person had the baby. She shrank back and let him hold him.

"He's learned to laugh," Cal said. "I wondered when that might happen."

"He loves you," Jess said, fingering her necklace. "How was the trip?"

"Wonderful. My brother is married and building a new house for his bride." Cal stopped, wondering if now was the time to say something. The others had wandered away, though once he caught Livvy looking back.

"All things are forgiven then?" Jess asked.

"Yep, I thank the Lord for that."

I know you missed Charlie, but did you miss me even a little bit? Jess wanted to ask.

"And how about you?"

"Oh, we heard just yesterday. A preacher is putting us on his circuit. He'll be here the end of summer."

"Hey, now that's great news."

❧

A preacher could marry us. But she's wearing that necklace. It's just a matter of time until she moves back to Kansas.

"I'll continue teaching the Sunday school class since everyone wants me to do that," Jess said. "And three more families are moving in. Pell's Valley is growing fast."

"What else is happening?" Cal asked. He wanted her to say how much she had missed him, but that wasn't going to be.

"I'm also giving more reading lessons, and Emma has picked up two students to learn the piano. We may have a school."

"A school?" Cal shook his head. "And all this happened in one week? Maybe I should go away more often." But even as he said it, he knew he wouldn't. He didn't want to go away. His life was here. With Jess. And Charlie.

"We need a school," Jess said. "I'll apply to teach. That's what I wanted to do before my parents died. But it was up to me to keep the farm going."

"You'll make a fine teacher," Cal said. "Look how much you've taught the Downing children and Emma and now Howard, you say. I'd better head out to the ranch, see how Henry's getting along. But first I need to get the wagon and unload some wood I brought." He leaned over and kissed the baby's forehead, then paused. He wanted more than anything to take Jess into his arms, but he knew he couldn't face her turning away, and surely she would if she still loved Brady.

"I'll see you on Sunday."

❧

Jess watched Cal head to the livery stable. She had almost grabbed him and pulled him close, but her one free hand didn't move. Charlie leaned over then and tugged at the necklace. She freed his hands and headed for home. Cal seemed different somehow, and she wondered what it meant. Was he going to return to Montana, though he made no mention of it, or had he realized he was still in love with the memory of his dead wife?

Once again she thought of returning to Kansas, but she wanted to stay here. She'd made so many friends and loved the people. She'd miss Emma, who was always there to talk to. She knew her friend would stop by later today and ask her what happened, ask her if she'd said anything to Cal. She'd have to tell her again that the words froze inside her, that he acted differently and she was sure he didn't love her.

Jess stepped into the general store to buy powdered milk. Livvy was talking at the end of the far aisle. A girl her age had moved to town, and they'd become friends overnight.

"Are you going to see him again soon?" the newcomer asked.

"As soon as I can."

Livvy had a boyfriend? Of course it was possible. Then Jess remembered the stagecoach driver and how he had stayed over an hour or so his last time in town.

Jess rang the bell, announcing she was ready to pay.

A red-faced Livvy ran down the aisle. "Oh, Jess, I'm sorry. I didn't hear you come in." She leaned over and tweaked Charlie's cheek.

"I know," Jess said. "I could tell."

"You didn't hear me talking—"

Jess smiled. "Well, just a few things."

"Oh, I'm so embarrassed. You won't tell anyone?"

Her friend walked past the counter and out the door. "See

you," she called over her shoulder.

Jess smiled again. "Why—and who—would I tell?"

"My father for one." Her eyes grew wide. "He doesn't want me to date anyone like a stagecoach driver. Says he'd be gone all the time, and it'd be a miserable life."

"And maybe it would be."

Soon Jess left the store, still chuckling to herself. If she couldn't be lucky in love, she could spur on someone else. It was the least she could do.

Cal didn't want to leave, but he knew he must. He hadn't spoken his true feelings to Jess. He'd rehearsed a speech repeatedly on the train. He *knew* what he wanted to say, so why hadn't he?

"Well, Dover, I think it's going to be just you and me living out on the ranch. I'll have a nice house, and I've ordered some furniture. But other than a milk cow or two and maybe one day a dog that will help with the cattle drive, it'll be us."

Dover whinnied as if he understood, and Cal gave him a few oats he had stashed in the saddlebag.

He was eager to see Henry. He'd given him a job to do with a hammer and a few nails. He was fifteen, and when Cal was that age, he could build a fence, herd the cows, and do any other job his father needed.

Jess. He couldn't get her off his mind. Why hadn't he gone ahead and asked about Brady? Asked if he was coming for a visit? If she was going back to Kansas? And if she'd said yes, what would he have said then? *Oh, that's nice?*

Words never came easily for him. He remembered as a kid riding all day on the back of a horse. He could retreat to his favorite spots. His brother, Tom, was much more talkative. It was Tom who had gone into the café and invited Millie to come to supper. Cal didn't know how to court. He hadn't known then, and he didn't know now. Millie had talked away the night, and he'd fallen in love with her sweet nature. When she asked once if he was going to stay a bachelor, he'd somehow found the right words to tell her no, that he would like it if she would be a rancher's wife. Not *his* wife, but a rancher's wife. She'd understood and had taken his hand and said, "If that was a proposal, the answer is yes."

Millie hadn't been shy in most ways, and Jess wasn't shy in any way as far as he had figured out. She made decisions, like insisting on the Christmas Eve service for the town, saying they needed a church, and later saying she could teach Sunday school once the building was finished.

That was why he knew she didn't think of him as anything more than a good friend. She was grateful he'd saved Charlie's life, grateful he'd buried Abby and said a prayer, grateful he'd agreed to read the Scripture on Christmas Eve.

Gratefulness wasn't the same as love. And he wanted someone to love him so completely that it wouldn't matter if the sun came up the next day as long as they had each other.

☙

Cal could see Henry sitting by the campfire. When the boy saw Cal, he jumped to his feet. "Hello!" he called out.

"Hello," Cal said. "Son, how's it been out here all by yourself?"

Henry's eyes sparkled. "Fine, Mr. Rutledge. Had no problems. But you know something?"

Cal shook his head. "No, what?"

"You need a dog."

Cal laughed. "I was thinking the same thing on the trip back here. Saw the old collie that used to round up the cattle when I was a kid and got to hankering for one." He slipped off his horse and stretched his muscles. "Suppose I could order one and the train could bring it in."

"What kind of dog?" Henry shaded his eyes against the afternoon sun.

"Don't rightly know. Maybe a collie, but any ol' mutt would be good."

Henry shook his head. "Don't know about a collie, but there're some cute dogs over at the Black ranch west of town.

They're still pups, but the owner—" He looked away.

"The owner—?" Cal wanted him to finish the sentence.

"He's mean to 'em."

"Mean?" Cal couldn't imagine being mean to a helpless animal.

"Yeah, takes a stick to 'em. They look purty hungry, too."

"Do you think he'd sell me one?"

"Bet he'd give 'em all to you."

"Don't rightly think I need more than one. Unless Jess wants one."

"I'd like to own one, but I know Ma'd say no. We have enough mouths to feed as it is."

Cal nodded. "Thanks for telling me. I'll check into it once I'm back in town."

"I put those boards up on that one wall," Henry said. "I got more done than you asked for."

"That's great. I owe you more money than we agreed on then."

"Nah, don't want more money. I'd do anything for you, Mr. Rutledge."

Cal's heart warmed as he reached over and clapped the boy's shoulder. "Son, I'm grateful for your help."

Henry beamed. "And there's something else—"

"And what might that be?"

"I like how you call me son."

Cal looked at the young man. "Doesn't your pa ever call you that?"

"No, sir. He don't call me anything, except sometimes when he's mad."

"Well, I'm guessing I call you that because you're the kind of son I hope to have someday."

After a supper of dried beef, Cal brought up the subject of the wood. "You know, I've been thinking I need some extra help with something I want built."

"Sure, Mr. Rutledge. What would that be?"

"Pews for our church. Think you could help me with that?"

Henry's eyes widened. "Never done nothin' like that before—"

"But you're willing to try." It was a statement, not a question. The boy nodded. "If you show me what to do."

"Then it's settled. We'll get busy tomorrow."

They called it a night. Henry stayed out under the stars, wrapped in a bedroll, and Cal decided to sleep out there, too, instead of in the lean-to.

The boy had managed well. He'd keep him on to help with the cattle later. And he'd get a dog soon. Why then couldn't Cal sleep?

Jess. Always Jess. He could be stubborn, too. He'd heard about men fighting for a woman, and though he never thought he could do that, he was beginning to change his mind. Cal spent the night talking to Dover and the stars in the clear, blue-black sky.

⁂

It was early when Cal and Henry arrived back in Pell's Valley. Once in town they rode out to the Black ranch. The man who owned the place wasn't home, but his wife listened to Cal's request.

"What'd you give me for one of 'em?" she asked.

Cal looked at the scrawny dogs—probably no more than three months old. One, a black and white mongrel that looked like a shepherd mix, licked his hand, while another, brown with white spots and a wide face, wagged his tail, watching him as if he thought Cal might have something to eat. "I think fifty cents for two."

"Sold!"

"This one is yours, son." Cal pointed to the one with white spots. "He seems to like you."

"But Ma will—"

"I'm keeping both of them, but one is yours when you come out to work on the ranch. I'll be needing you most of the time. You think that'd be okay by your folks?"

Henry's eyes lit up. "Oh, yes, sir. I'm sure it will be just fine."

"What're we going to name these two?"

"I reckon I like the name Skip," Henry said.

Cal laughed. "Skip it is, then. I'm partial to Rusty for the other one."

❦

After Henry obtained permission to return to the ranch, the two began working on the pews. Cal measured while Henry sawed. Together they pounded nails. They both liked the end results, though they had finished only two by Sunday.

"Sure is beautiful wood," Cal said. "Takes longer than I thought though."

Henry nodded. "Yep."

"I guess we won't make it in for Sunday school," Cal said. "I hope that's okay with you."

Henry smiled. "I think we need to finish these first."

❦

Jess was eager for Sunday to come since she figured Cal would come to church. Every time the door opened, she glanced up expectantly. He was just late, she thought. He'd come in after a while. She knew he wouldn't stay away from seeing Charlie for long. What if he was sick?

Henry hadn't returned either, so she figured they were building more on the house.

Jess took Charlie over to Emma's for supper, which had become a weekly custom.

"I see Cal didn't make it," Emma said.

"It's a long way," Jess said, setting the table once she had secured Charlie in the high chair.

"I don't think that'd stop him."

"Maybe he's sick."

"No, don't think he is."

"Can we talk about something else?" Jess asked.

"Why? Are you uncomfortable talking about this?"

"Well, yes, you know I am."

"One of you has to swallow your pride and speak out. I can't imagine your being silent." Emma finished putting the food on the table.

"I've had no encouragement." Jess mounded the mashed potatoes on her plate but knew she wouldn't finish them.

"Cal's shy; you're not."

"And he still loves his wife."

"I don't think so."

"He loves Charlie, and that's the main reason he comes around."

"Sure, he loves Charlie, but it goes further than that." Emma sighed. "I think he thinks you're still in love with Brady. You wear that necklace he gave you at Christmas."

Jess's fingers touched the necklace. "*This?* You think this is the necklace Brady gave me?"

"Isn't it?"

"No. It was Abby's. I found it in her belongings. After Brady left I started wearing this one."

"Looks like the one from Brady."

"But it's smaller." Jess fingered the chain. "I like to wear it. It makes me feel closer to Abby." Jess shook her head. "I can't believe you thought. . . And if you thought that—"

"Cal did also."

"Oh, Emma. I had no idea."

"Now will you say something? Or take it off—or wear it under your shirt."

That night Jess slept better than she had for a long time. She'd been in love with Cal Rutledge for nearly four months, and she was finally going to do something about it. She was more than ready to be the wife of a rancher, and she wanted Cal Rutledge more than she'd wanted anything in her entire life. Would he come into town, or would she have to go to him?

❧

Cal felt bad about missing the Sunday school class. The six

pews were finally finished, and he could hardly wait to put them in the church. The outside of his new house was also nearly completed. All he needed now was the furniture and a woman's touch, and he hoped to remedy that. He'd ask Jess to marry him when he went into town on Friday. His furniture would be coming in on the train then.

Henry helped with the sign, and again Cal was pleased with his help. He was a hard worker and would definitely make a good ranch hand.

Thursday they rose early and soon had the wagon loaded with the pews. Henry climbed up on the seat next to Cal.

"I can't wait to see what Miss Jess says."

"Yep, she'll be mighty surprised."

"Are the dogs going with us?"

Cal nodded. "Can't leave 'em here. Not yet. Maybe when they're a bit older it'd be okay." He leaned down and patted both. They were starting to fill out and become handsome dogs. He wondered what Jess would think. If she wanted one, he'd give her Rusty.

The ride in was slow going. Dover wasn't used to carrying so much.

"Probably should get another horse so I can have a pair," Cal said.

"What kind will you get?"

"Maybe another buckskin. I'm partial to them."

The boy sat back and whittled on a piece of scrap wood. "Someday I'm getting me a horse, too."

"Yep, I figure you will."

They rode on in silence, but Cal's mind was working. He missed Jess's smile and Charlie's toothless grin. *Lord,* he prayed, *You know the desires of my heart. I don't think You'll let me down now. And if Jess returns to Kansas, she was never mine to begin with.*

They arrived at the church and moved out all the chairs. Livvy heard the commotion and hurried over to see.

"Pews!" she cried out. "I declare, won't Jess be surprised!"

Cal nodded. "Yep. That's what I'm figuring on."

"They're just *beautiful*." She touched one, then sat down. "Sits nice, too."

Henry watched her and grinned.

"One more thing," Cal said. "Henry, get the sign."

Soon the sign was in place by the side that faced the street. "Looks plumb fancy, if I do say so myself."

Henry kept grinning.

"That's it," Cal said, looking at Henry. "Unless you want to get Miz Wilcox and ask her to come and see the pews."

"Yes, I'll do that."

"Don't tell her why now," Cal said. "We want it to be a surprise."

"I know."

"Take the horse and wagon."

Cal paced back and forth by the church. He felt like a young boy with his first pony.

"Now what are you so excited about that it couldn't wait another minute?" Jess hopped down from the wagon, then reached over and took Charlie from Henry. "Henry said I had to come *now*."

"Yep. It's important all right. You'll see."

A few people hung around the outside of the church. He winked at Henry. "Open the door, son."

Jess stepped inside, and her eyes widened. She said nothing as she stood and stared. Then she reached out to touch the beautiful wood.

"Pews! Just what this church needed. But where did you get them?" She looked at Cal, then back at Henry, who was still beaming.

"We made 'em!"

"*Made* them?"

"Sure did."

Jess sat in one, her grin widening. "They sit really nice. But I can't believe it."

"Got the oak from a friend in Montana. He insisted I take it—he can't work anymore."

"That was kind of him." Jess clasped her hands. "I can hardly wait until Sunday for everyone to see."

"Won't be no surprise by then," Henry said. "Everyone will hear about it and come to see before."

"And that isn't all," Cal said next. "One more surprise, Miz Wilcox. And Henry is responsible for the workmanship on this."

They walked around the side of the building toward the road. The sign declaring "Pell's Valley Community Church" shone in the morning sunshine.

"Oh!" Jess looked at the sign, then over at Henry. "You carved the letters?"

"Sure did—that is, after Mr. Rutledge told me how to spell." Several people laughed then.

"All we need now is a preacher," Jess said, "and he'll be here in a few months."

Cal helped Jess back into the wagon, then handed over the chortling baby. "I'll take you back home, and maybe we can have a cup of coffee to celebrate."

"I thought you might come for coffee." Jess smiled. "And I have biscuits left over from yesterday if you want some."

"I'd love some."

Minutes later Cal watched Jess flitting about the small kitchen, and soon his coffee was in front of him with a saucer holding two biscuits already buttered.

"I hope it's okay that I buttered the biscuits."

He nodded. "It's fine, Jess."

She held Charlie close and sat in the rocking chair across the room from him. As she held the baby, she rocked a bit, her toe giving a little push when Charlie cooed. It was as if he were asking her to rock more. She hugged him and looked at Cal.

"I missed you on Sunday."

"And I missed being here." Cal's hands, needing to be busy, crept around the rim of his cowboy hat. The felt was old, and he needed a new one. He could have bought one in Montana, but he hadn't thought of it then.

"Is your house finished?" she asked.

"Yep, pretty close."

"And do I remember hearing that you're only waiting for furniture now?"

"Coming in on tomorrow's train."

"What's coming?"

"Table. Chairs. A rocking chair. A bed—" He glanced up. Their gazes met and held.

"I'm not good at this sort of thing, Jess. I mean, it's not me. How do I know—" His voice cracked as he looked back at his hat and began the motion again, turning it with his hands, bending the brim a bit.

"I'm sure the furniture is going to be nice."

"But there needs to be more."

"You can always add to it later. Sounds as if you have the most important items."

"Yeah, well. . ."

Oh, help me, Lord. This isn't going well at all. I can't say what I want to say. I feel all tongue-tied and stupid-like.

"I've come to a few decisions myself," Jess began.

Cal's heart sank. It was coming now. She'd tell him she was returning to Kansas. He took a deep breath and looked over. His hat fell to the floor. The necklace was gone. It wasn't around her neck. Did it mean what he hoped it meant?

"What happened to the necklace Brady gave you?"

Jess smiled. "Emma said you thought I was still wearing Brady's necklace."

"And you weren't?"

"No, it was Abby's."

"It looked the same."

Jess felt her heart beat faster. "Yes, I know. But it was among

Abby's possessions you gave me. Remember it was broken? I took the chain off the one from Brady."

"I thought you loved Brady."

"I never loved Brady."

"I thought you were going back to Kansas."

"I know. I thought about going back to Kansas, but I can't."

"Can't?"

"My life is here in Pell's Valley. Where Charlie's life began."

"Oh, if only you knew how many times I prayed for that. If only you knew how much I wanted to tell you things—"

"Tell me now, Cal. I want to hear them now."

Charlie let out a squeal and pulled one of Jess's curls. Her hair seemed more mussed than usual, but he liked it that way. Fact was, he liked everything about her.

"Well, you have the church going now, the teaching, and people around here sure like you."

"Yes, Cal. Some people do."

"And I'd miss you something awful if you left."

"You'd miss Charlie, too."

"Yep, that I would. It's the truth." *Why can't I just get this over with?* "I have the house now—"

"So you've said."

"The furniture is coming—and yeah, guess I already said that, too. And, well, a bed isn't a bed if you don't have someone to share it with." He looked up again. "Jess, I'm not much, but I'm going to try to do better, and I want you to marry me."

There. It's out. I've finally said it. Why doesn't she say something? She could at least hurry up if she has to turn me down.

Jess stared at him for a moment, then let out a gasp, handed Charlie to him, and ran into the kitchen.

Cal held Charlie close, not noticing that he was tugging on his beard. He heard dishes clinking and a cupboard door closing.

a.

Jess closed a cupboard door, wiped the counter, and looked out the window. *Why am I acting this way? Why did I run out of the room? I love him, Lord. You know I do. Why is it so difficult to tell him so?*

"Can I help you with something?"

Cal stood in the doorway, holding Charlie close. "I didn't mean to be out of line, and if you still love Brady, I understand. I know you don't like the desert. You told me more than once, and I just thought—"

"Cal, will you just be quiet?" Jess turned with a look in her eye. "I thought you were never going to ask me. I thought you still loved your wife and the only reason you came around was because of Charlie. I have loved you from the moment you paused by the train and asked if I needed help. Oh, I fought the feeling, but it was there—it's been there all this time—and God kept telling me to be patient. Emma kept saying to tell you, that you needed to know—"

"Oh, Jess." He was across the room in a second, pulling her to him, with Charlie between them.

"I never dared hope. You're elegant. I'm just a cowboy—"

"And cowboys need to be loved."

"Yep, I reckon you're right."

She lifted her face to him. "There's just one thing."

"Tell me." *I don't even care what it is, Lord. She feels so right in my arms, and I'm so happy my heart is going to burst right out of my shirt.*

Jess grinned. "I'm wondering. Whose house are we going to live in?"

epilogue

The cooling winds of early September rolled in off the hills. The first snow would soon hit, but Cal was ready for it this year.

The new preacher had come on the morning train. The service would be held at noon. Every pew was filled, and chairs were placed along the side. The one-room church couldn't have held another soul. Emma pounded out songs on the old piano while the children sang a song she had taught them.

Jess, in the back room of the general store, adjusted the veil she'd made. A long, white, full-skirted gown in a sprigged calico touched the floor gracefully. Jess's cheeks were red as Livvy checked to see if every button was buttoned, every hair in place. She pushed her toward the door. "You come right after I leave now. They're waiting. You're five minutes late as it is."

Livvy, dressed in a dainty rose pattern, left the store, walking slowly across the street and into the church, and stopped in the front. Emma hit the chords for the "Wedding March," and everyone stood.

Jess came in carrying her bouquet of sagebrush blooms and reached for Cal's hand as he moved to stand beside her. Cal, in a new white shirt and denim jacket, stood tall, his best man, Henry Downing, next to him.

Elias Downing, sitting at the back of the church with the rest of his family, clapped suddenly. Jess smiled. She certainly never thought she'd see him in church, but if it took a wedding, so be it. Jess fought back the tears as she looked at Cal.

Lord, pinch me. Am I really here? About to take vows with the man I love more than life itself? And to think I came here to Pell's Valley less than a year ago and found the desires of my heart.

The music stopped, and Preacher Davidson stepped before them. "Dearly beloved, we gather today to witness the union of this man and this woman."

Suddenly they heard laughing in the back of the room and turned around. Baby Charlie jumped up and down in Dorothy's lap. Jess giggled—she couldn't help it—and Cal winked.

They repeated their vows, and then Cal was kissing her. And her heart rose to new heights as she kissed him back.

"Well done!" Preacher Davidson declared. Then everyone clapped as he pronounced them "man and wife." Emma played the piano as everyone left for the reception in the back room of the general store.

Tonight they would stay in Jess's house, but tomorrow Cal would transport his wife and son to his new home.

TOM'S BUTTERMILK PIE

½ cup butter
2 cups sugar
2 tsp. vanilla extract
3 eggs
3 tablespoons flour

¼ tsp. salt
1 cup buttermilk
½-1 cup chopped pecans
1 deep unbaked pie crust

Preheat oven to 300°. In large bowl, cream butter and sugar until fluffy. Mixture should not be grainy. Blend in vanilla. Add eggs, one at a time. Combine flour and salt; add a small amount at a time. Add buttermilk. Sprinkle nuts in bottom on piecrust and pour buttermilk mixture over top. Bake 1½ hours or until top browns. Best served at room temperature.

A Letter To Our Readers

Dear Reader:
In order that we might better contribute to your reading enjoyment, we would appreciate your taking a few minutes to respond to the following questions. We welcome your comments and read each form and letter we receive. When completed, please return to the following:

Fiction Editor
Heartsong Presents
PO Box 719
Uhrichsville, Ohio 44683

1. Did you enjoy reading *Sagebrush Christmas* by Birdie L. Etchison?
   ❏ Very much! I would like to see more books by this author!
   ❏ Moderately. I would have enjoyed it more if

   _____

   _____

   _____

2. Are you a member of **Heartsong Presents**? ❏ Yes ❏ No
   If no, where did you purchase this book? _____

   _____

3. How would you rate, on a scale from 1 (poor) to 5 (superior), the cover design? _____

4. On a scale from 1 (poor) to 10 (superior), please rate the following elements.

   ____ Heroine   ____ Plot
   ____ Hero   ____ Inspirational theme
   ____ Setting   ____ Secondary characters

5. These characters were special because? _____

_____

_____

6. How has this book inspired your life? _____

_____

_____

7. What settings would you like to see covered in future
   Heartsong Presents books? _____

_____

_____

8. What are some inspirational themes you would like to see
   treated in future books? _____

_____

_____

9. Would you be interested in reading other **Heartsong
   Presents** titles?   ❑ Yes   ❑ No

10. Please check your age range:
    ❑ Under 18   ❑ 18-24
    ❑ 25-34   ❑ 35-45
    ❑ 46-55   ❑ Over 55

Name _____

Occupation _____

Address _____

City, State, Zip _____

Hearts♥ng

HEARTSONG PRESENTS TITLES AVAILABLE NOW:

(If ordering from this page, please remember to include it with the order form.)

— Presents —

Great Inspirational Romance at a Great Price!

Heartsong Presents books are inspirational romances in contemporary and historical settings, designed to give you an enjoyable, spirit-lifting reading experience. You can choose wonderfully written titles from some of today's best authors like Peggy Darty, Sally Laity, DiAnn Mills, Colleen L. Reece, Debra White Smith, and many others.

When ordering quantities less than twelve, above titles are $2.97 each.
Not all titles may be available at time of order.